DRAGON GUARD PROTECTOR

Dragon Guard of the Northern Isles Book 5

ALICIA MONTGOMERY

Copyright © 2022 Alicia Montgomery
www.aliciamontgomeryauthor.com
first electronic publication March 2022

Edited by LaVerne Clark
Cover by Jacqueline Sweet
031922

ALSO BY ALICIA MONTGOMERY

A Witch in Time

Highland Wolf

Daughter of the Dragon

Shadow Wolf

A Touch of Magic

Heart of the Wolf

THE BLACKSTONE MOUNTAIN SERIES

The Blackstone Dragon Heir

The Blackstone Bad Dragon

The Blackstone Bear

The Blackstone Wolf

The Blackstone Lion

The Blackstone She-Wolf

The Blackstone She-Bear

The Blackstone She-Dragon

BLACKSTONE RANGERS SERIES

Blackstone Ranger Chief

Blackstone Ranger Charmer

Blackstone Ranger Hero

Blackstone Ranger Rogue

Blackstone Ranger Guardian

Blackstone Ranger Scrooge

Dragon Guard of the Northern Isles

Dragon Guard Warrior

Dragon Guard Scholar

Dragon Guard Knight

Dragon Guard Fighter

Dragon Guard Protector

Dragon Guard Crusader

PROLOGUE

About three years ago ...

The rhythmic crashing of the waves against the shore was the only sound Stein could hear for miles. But the tension in the air was palpable, and every dragon shifter on the beach could feel it hanging over them like a heavy curtain. The enemy forces were on the way, and they had to be ready to defend their country and its people.

"What do you think is going through Aleksei's head?"

Niklas's voice broke through Stein's reverie like breaking glass.

Who knows? Stein answered through the mind link that connected every dragon—in their case, water dragon—of the same kind.

As usual, neither Stein's clipped tone nor his fierce stare directed into the distance could discourage the gregarious Niklas as he continued. "Gods, he must be having a rough time. I can't even imagine what he must be feeling right now."

"He nearly lost his father, of course he's having a rough time." The somber statement came from the man beside Niklas. Although they were identical in every way, Gideon was much quieter and more pensive than his twin.

"I get it," Niklas said. "At least now he and Sybil are finally mated. That should help him through this."

Stein's head snapped toward Niklas. *The prince and female are mated?* The idea jarred him so much he practically shouted it into his companions' minds.

"Stein, dude." Niklas winced and rubbed his temple. "I've had enough screaming in my mind for one day. Tone it down."

You are certain? Stein interrogated.

"Yeah, I'm sure. Right, Gideon?"

Gideon nodded. "She spoke to us via the mind link, which confirms their status as bonded mates."

"More like screamed out graphic sex details I never wanted to know," Niklas moaned. "It's not the best way to find out, but I'm happy for them. I know Sybil was reluctant and all, but no one can stop fate, can they?"

The words made Stein's blood freeze in his veins.

"She's not going to be very happy once she's out of the basement," Gideon reminded him.

Basement?

Niklas's blonde eyebrows furrowed. "Right before we went to the war room, Sybil insisted in coming along and fighting. Aleksei wasn't having it, so he locked her in the basement with Lady Willa."

Stein raised an eyebrow. *Whyever for?*

"To protect her, of course."

"That's the most idiotic thing I've heard." Indeed, it sounded so preposterous to Stein, he had to say it aloud.

"You do know that's our future king you're talking about," Gideon pointed out.

Yes. But Sybil Lennox is hardly a wilting flower. She may have grown up privileged, but she is no spoiled princess. She is strong on the inside and out. And she is a mountain dragon, lest you two forget.

The twins gave him identical slack-jawed expressions, so he continued. *We could use her in this fight. Her fire alone could turn the tide for us. To have her locked up when she could help us is preposterous and a waste.*

"That's true, but she's also the future queen of the Northern Isles," Gideon reminded them. "And mate to Aleksei. If anything happens to her, he'd be devastated."

Niklas's face turned serious. "I can't even imagine what it would be like to find your mate and lose her."

Stein swallowed the lump growing in his throat. Thankfully, before anyone else could say anything, their prince's voice rang through their mental link.

Ready! Aleksei commanded.

A group of ships appeared on the horizon, and they were fast approaching. Every single dragon on the beach replied to their prince with an affirmative. Clearing his mind of all distraction, Stein grit his teeth and readied for the battle ahead.

Attack! came the prince's command.

Loud war cries pierced the air as the men hurtled toward the ocean, transforming into their dragon forms. Stein easily slid into his animal's skin, his body elongating into a large creature covered in blue and black scales. The humongous

3

dragon's scarred body dove into the waves and headed straight for the enemy ships.

I'll take the lead ship, Prince Aleksei stated *And you take your positions and attack at will.*

There was no need for more instructions after that. The Dragon Guard and the Royal Dragon Navy had their orders and faced their enemies full on.

The battle raged as the dragons clashed with the forces of the Knights of Aristaeum. Stein relished every moment of it using his own pent-up rage to fuel his dragon and crush as many boats as he could. In fact, he was so caught up that he didn't hear the din above him until he felt the heat of fire as lava spilled into the cool ocean, the steam billowing off the waves. Small objects began to drop around him like baseball-sized raindrops, and the smell of burning metal assaulted his nose.

What in the gods' names ...?

Stein paused and looked up.

Thousands of drones flew overhead, all of them headed for the mainland. However, something large and gold and shimmery followed them, its great maw opening as fire spewed out from its mouth.

Sybil Lennox.

Now *that* was a queen.

He was entranced for a moment as fierce pride rose in him. He knew that Sybil was fierce and strong; the gods surely would not have given their future king a weak mate.

Though some might think that the gods could sometimes make mistakes when it comes to such things.

... Do what you can to assist my mate. I'll be right beside you.

Stein caught the tail end of the conversation, not really sure if it was meant for him. But it seemed Sybil needed some help, so he pushed his dragon up, flapping its wings to hurtle himself out of the water. The mighty creature dashed toward the hoard of drones, ready to swat down as many as it could when Stein saw a smaller group break off from the swarm and head west.

To the capital city.

A cold, icy feeling gripped Stein. It was a feeling he was unfamiliar with because he thought it banished from his very being, when he decided that no one would ever have such power over him again.

Fear.

Without another thought, he turned his dragon's body to chase after the drones.

Stein! Thoralf, Captain of the Dragon Guard, called. *Where are you going?*

He couldn't ignore his captain, so he sent out a warning through their mind link. *A few drones broke off from the hive and are headed to the city. I need to get there before they destroy the city and hurt anyone.*

Before they hurt her.

If there was one lesson her mother never let Lady Vera Solveigson forget, it was this: Being nice will never get you what you want. It didn't matter who you had to push or claw out of your way, but you can't let others stop you from achieving your goals.

And just like her dear deceased mother, Vera always got what she wanted.

Growing up as the only daughter of the Northern Isles' richest and most powerful jarl ensured she always had the best things: the most expensive toys, finest designer clothes, exotic vacations, and the best schooling from the top schools in London, Paris, and Switzerland.

So, when she finally came back to the Northern Isles two years ago, she decided she *had* to have the best from home too: Crown Prince Aleksei.

Vera thought he'd always been handsome and dashing. The fact that he was a dragon shifter never bothered her; she was from the Northern Isles after all. In her mind, it made perfect sense—him, the only son and heir to the throne of the kingdom, and her, daughter of the king's most powerful adviser and ally.

For the last two years, she'd done everything she could to catch his attention and stay on his radar. Attended every boring event and dull dinner at the palace, made conversation with Prince Aleksei when she got the chance, and even bribing the royal social secretary for his whereabouts for every official function in the city.

The crown prince had always been polite, dancing with her at balls and conversing at dinners. He might not have been as warm as she'd like, but since he was a public figure, he had to keep his emotions to himself. Vera knew she only had to be patient and bide her time. One day, they'd be alone and he would have the chance to declare his interest in her.

But now, that ... *woman* had ruined it.

Vera scoffed. Sybil whatever-her-name-was. An *American*, of all things! Sister of a dear friend and personal guest of the prince. *Hah!* The Northern Isles' location was a secret to the bigger world, and there was no way the royal family would have invited just anyone. No, Vera knew there was something different about this woman.

Even though her mother had been dead for six years now, her voice rang clear in Vera's head.

Do not let this usurper ruin two years of hard work, Vera. You know what you need to do.

A simple switch of the place cards at dinner the other night ensured Vera would be able to keep the prince away from that outsider. But still, when they were all supposed to gather in the drawing room for after-dinner drinks, the prince and Sybil were noticeably absent.

Vera, you weak fool! This is your fault. Did you really think you could keep the crown prince's attentions? You're too ugly and fat. Who knows what they could be doing right now?

It made Vera want to scream as she imagined the prince and that woman together.

Of course, as of the moment, she knew they couldn't be up to anything because of the nationwide lockdown ordered by the Royal Dragon Navy.

Vera sighed and propped her chin on her hands as she sat by her bedroom window. It was a beautiful, clear fall day in the Northern Isles, but she couldn't even go out and enjoy it. Apparently there was some kind of security breach with the magical veil that protected the islands, so everyone was ordered to stay inside.

She and her father had been having lunch when their security team rushed in and told them of the lockdown. It wasn't unusual; they had drills like this a few times a year. However, as she had been whisked away to her room, the serious, hushed tones of her father and the head of security told her something else was going on.

That had been an hour ago, and she hadn't heard anything else since. And to think, she'd had the perfect excuse to go to the palace today. She'd overheard during dinner that the Queen's Trust, Prince Aleksei's dear departed mother's charity foundation, were looking for volunteers. She was going to march in there and offer her services, sign up for every committee, and if she had to—kiss and serve soup to every ragamuffin and guttersnipe on the street.

"Stupid lockdown! Why the—" Vera frowned as she spied three vehicles making their way up the driveway to their mansion. They weren't just normal cars or vans. The bright yellow and black buses chugging toward the house were emblazoned on the side with the name of the nearby elementary school.

What on earth was going on?

Dashing out of her room, Vera made her way downstairs to the main hall where her father stood in the foyer, speaking to a middle-aged woman dressed in a dull gray suit as a stream of children entered their home.

"Vera," her father greeted, his face fraught with worry. "What are you doing here?" He shook his head. "Never mind. I was going to fetch you anyway to take you down to the basement shelter."

"Sh-shelter?" Her hand went to her chest. "What do you mean, shelter, and who are these people?"

"My lady." The woman gave her a respectful nod. "My name is Elsa Midrad, principal of King Hakkonnen Elementary. Thank you for offering your home as a shelter for the children during these trying times. We have our youngest students here, from the pre-kindergarten classes." She patted a young boy who stopped in front of them. "Go on, Johann, follow your friends ..."

Vera frowned. "Father, what's going on?"

"Dear ... this isn't a drill." He gently placed a comforting hand on Vera's shoulder. "We are under attack by enemies of our country. The prince, the Dragon Guard, and the Royal Navy are battling them now."

A hand covered her mouth. "No ... Prince Aleksei ..."

"Will prevail," he said, confident. "But we must do our part. I have offered to shelter as many people as we can handle here, as well as set up an overflow for the hospital should it be needed." The nearing sound of a siren punctuated his words. "Ah, that's probably the backup staff from Odelia General. I've instructed the security team to lead them to the rear entrance so as not to alarm the children. I must go and greet them. Please, Vera, go take shelter in the basement now." The urgency in her father's voice was unmistakable.

"Y-yes, Pappa."

She watched him rush out, her heart hammering in her chest. This was serious. Because of the secretive nature of their country and the presence of the water dragons, everyone in the Northern Isles grew up learning drills and memorizing emergency plans in case they ever did get attacked. And now it was coming true. For the first time in her life, she was truly frightened.

"My lady?"

She turned to Principal Midrad. "Yes?"

"Shouldn't you be heading down to the shelter?"

"I ..." She supposed she should do that. But something

twisted in her stomach. As if her breakfast hadn't settled in properly. Like something felt ... off.

Remember what I told you, Vera. Only look out for yourself.

"Principal Midrad, is there anything I can do?" Vera found herself saying.

Midrad glanced around her. "Looks like the first bus is done. I should go out and start unloading the children from the second one. If you wouldn't mind, could you stay here and ensure the next batch of children that come in don't stray and instead head toward the right direction?"

"Of course." It seemed like an easy enough request. Vera knew nothing about children. She knew someday she'd have some of her own, but after birthing them, she assumed she'd hand them over to a team of nannies so she could return to her social activities. It was how she had been raised, after all. How old were these children, anyway? She had no idea.

Vera started at the sound of footsteps, and more children started streaming inside, single file. "Er ... that way ... children," she called out, pointing to the hallway that led to the basement shelter. "Go on ... yes."

Most of them were quiet and somber, though some were wide-eyed as they surveyed their surroundings. She wondered what they were thinking and what Principal Midrad had told them. Did they think this was a drill or the real thing? Were they confused? Scared? Excited?

When one child—a dark-haired boy that was no taller than her waist—strayed from the line, she reached out and patted him on the head. "It's going to be all right." Gods, that sounded awkward. When was the last time she'd spoken to a child? Perhaps when she had been one herself.

Searching the room, she saw one of the maids take the hand of the little girl at the beginning of the line and lead them toward the kitchen where the entrance to the Solveigson bunker was located. *Oh, thank the gods.*

As more children came in, Vera simply did as she was told. "Stay in line now ... that's it ..." It didn't seem very hard at all, taking care of children. *I might even get used to this.* The stream of youngsters seemed never-ending with Midrad peeking in once through the doorway to let her know there was one last busload left.

When the last child walked through the door, Principal Midrad hurried in from behind. "Looks like we have all of them," she declared. "Lady Vera, thank you for your help."

"Principal Midrad! Principal Midrad!"

The principal's gaze shifted just over her shoulder. Turning around, Vera saw a blond boy dashing toward them.

"Kirk? What is it?"

The child took a deep breath, his puffed-up cheeks red from exertion. "Principal Midrad, Lisbet is missing!"

"Missing?" Midrad gasped. "Why did her buddy not say anything?"

"She-she didn't have a buddy," the boy confessed. "And she wasn't in my class so I didn't know until we were all down there. Please, you have to find her!"

"Calm down, Kirk." She brushed the tears away from his face. "Go back to your friends, and I shall head out and find her. My lady," she said to Vera. "You should take shelter as well."

Vera pressed her lips together. "But the child? Where will you look for her?"

"I saw her get on the bus." Midrad pursed her lips. "So

she must be here somewhere. Perhaps she's on the bus or broke off from the line as she was getting off." Her eyebrows knitted together. "Lisbet hasn't been quite the same since her father died last year. She's been mostly keeping to herself, and the other children tend to tease her a lot."

"How cruel." Vera curled her fists into her palms. "Principal Midrad, let me help you look for her."

You don't know this child, Vera. Stop acting foolish.

"You want to help?"

"Of course. No one knows the grounds and the estate better than I do."

"But you should take shelter—"

Vera raised a hand to stop her. "She can't have gone far. I'm sure she's just somewhere nearby."

"I—"

What are you doing, Vera?

"Please. Let me help."

Midrad blew out a breath. "If you insist, my lady. But if it's taking too long, please go inside. I don't want anything to happen to you."

"I'll be fine," she assured her. "I'll take the east side and you take the west, then we'll circle to the back and meet by the dragon fountain in, let's say ... fifteen minutes? That should be enough time to cover the perimeter of the house and find the girl."

"All right."

They headed outside together, down the grand marble steps, then separated at the bottom by the driveway. Vera headed to the right, making her way to the east side of the perimeter, but didn't get very far. She cursed as her heels sank into the gravel walkway. *I just got these from Milan last month*, she thought glumly. Stopping by one of the rows of rose bushes, she sighed and slipped them off her feet.

"*Achoo!*"

That had to be the girl. "Lisbet?" she called. "Lisbet, are you there?" Glancing around her, she followed the sound of rustling leaves and twigs just a few feet away, stepping through the gap between the bushes. Sure enough, she found a small figure crouched into a ball. "Are you Lisbet?"

The blonde head lifted, and wide blue eyes stared up at her, and the vulnerable expression on the child's face made something in Vera's chest crack. "I'm scared."

Vera sighed. "It's all right. So am I. But everything's going to be fine. The dragons will protect us."

"My m-mama ... she works in the capital, cleaning offices," she continued. "Do you think she is safe?"

Vera desperately wanted to tell her that her mother would be all right. But as she knew, no matter how much people thought their parents were immortal, it simply wasn't true. However, before she could find the right words, a loud buzzing sound made her pause and look up. "What in the gods—" She gasped.

In the distance, what looked like a dark swarm of birds were headed straight for them. Something inside her told her that she had to run. Without a second thought, Vera scooped the child up in her arms and made a mad dash to the house.

The ominous buzzing sound grew louder, and Lisbet kicked and struggled, making it difficult to run, so Vera halted to try and calm her down. "Please, *lilla du*," she soothed, hugging her tight and pressed her cheek to the child's temple. "We must get—"

A screeching sound interrupted her. The fierce howl made every hair on her body stand on end.

"Look!" Lisbet gasped, finger pointing to the sky.

Coming even faster toward them was a humungous winged creature, covered in scales in various shades of blue and black. Its mighty horned head swung back and forth as its wings flapped hard and overtook the swarm. Vera watched in horror as the dragon stopped right above the house and spread its wings, blocking the black swarm with its back. She crumpled to the ground, covering Lisbet's body with her own as the explosion made the ground shake.

Something dropped a few feet to her right, crashing down with a loud metallic crunch. From the wires and various electronic components, it looked like some kind of robot. *Or an explosive.* Quickly, she picked up Lisbet and dragged them both to the nearest tree, sheltering them from the rain of debris. To her horror, when her gaze turned skyward, the dragon flapped its wings helplessly, until it eventually stopped.

She didn't know why, but she let out a scream.

"No!" Her chest tightened at the sight of the dragon falling to earth. To her surprise, however, it quickly shrank, but that didn't make the sickening sound of a human body hitting the ground any less terrible. "Lisbet." She clutched the child's shoulders. "Go inside."

"But—"

"Please!" She smoothed the girl's mussed hair. "Your friends and Principal Midrad are looking for you."

"The dragon ... he saved us."

"I know, and I'll make sure he's safe, all right?"

Make sure he's safe? her mother's voice mocked.

Convinced, Lisbet nodded. "Yes, miss."

"Good." She gave the child her best approximation of a comforting smile before she ran off toward the house.

Straightening her shoulders, Vera rushed toward the fallen dragon. Though they weren't immortal, as far as she knew, dragon shifters were strong and could heal from most injuries. However, that explosion sounded and felt terribly powerful, and dread pooled in her stomach as she wondered what state the shifter would be in. She held her breath as she drew closer.

The now-human figure lay still, but thankfully fully intact. From what was left of his armor, Vera guessed he was one of the Dragon Guards who protected the royal family. Had she seen him before at the palace? She couldn't recall because she never did pay them any mind. The scars on his large body were old, though there were healing wounds on his massive back. Bile rose in her throat at the smell of singed flesh.

Get back inside, Vera. He's done his duty. He should be proud to die for his king and country.

Ignoring the voice, she carefully approached the fallen man and knelt down next to him.

Her breath hitched in her throat. His head was turned sidewards, so she could only make out his profile. His dark hair was cut short and shaved on the sides, but a long braid hung from the back. The strong lines on his face made him look fierce, even in sleep—or was he in a coma?

A strange pang echoed in her chest. Unable to help herself, she reached out toward his brow, but before she could even touch him, a humungous hand snaked out and caught her wrist.

She let out a cry of surprise and yanked her hand back. Attempted to, anyway, because he was so strong, she couldn't move an inch. His eyes flew open, and steely gray orbs stared right into her. A brief flash of surprise crossed his face, followed by another emotion she couldn't name.

"What ... are you ... doing?" His voice was low and gravelly, like he had just woken up after a deep sleep.

"Y-y-you fell," she replied, her voice shaky.

"Why ... are you ... out here?"

Why was she out here? "Look, there's no time for this, we need to get you inside before more of those ... things come back." Again, she tried to yank her hand away, but he wouldn't let go. "Release me at once!"

Those steely eyes pinned her. "You should have been inside," he growled. "Where it's safe. You could have been hurt!"

What was this man talking about? "You should get those wounds looked at. We have medical staff inside—"

"No." He released her, then pushed his hands on the ground, letting out a pained grunt as he attempted to get up. "I need to go back to the battle."

He stumbled forward, and Vera instinctively braced herself against his massive chest. Heat spread through her as she felt his bare skin on her cheeks and hands. She'd never touched a naked man in her life, after all.

"Careful!" she snapped when he attempted to push her away. It sounded harsh, even to her ears, but she'd never been in such a situation before. "Clumsy buffoon," she muttered.

"I must go," he grumbled as he attempted to disentangle himself from her.

"You're in no condition to leave," she stated. Gods help

her, she didn't know why she cared. He was a soldier. This was his duty. But the wounds on his back weren't fully healed yet, and from the way he placed most of his hulking weight on her, she could tell he was not doing well. "Come on."

Vera wrapped an arm around his trim waist, ignoring the way his rock-hard abdomen muscles jumped when her fingers clutched at him.

"Stop ... must ..."

She gritted her teeth and dragged him back toward the manor, heaving and grunting as he struggled against her like a weak kitten. Miraculously, she managed to haul him all the way to the front steps.

"Help!" she cried. "Please! I need help!" Relief rushed through her as two people dressed in scrubs hurried toward them. "He's hurt," she told one of the nurses.

"I am fine," the Dragon Guard snarled, but winced when the male nurse slipped an arm under him.

"Check his back," she told the female nurse. "It looks terrible."

"It's healing," he corrected. "And I told you, I am fine! Stop hounding me, woman!"

"Woman?" she cried in indignation. "How dare you? Do you know who I am?"

"Leave me alone," he shouted. "All of you."

"You stubborn oaf!"

"Nag," he shot back.

"Why I never—"

"My lady." The male nurse cleared his throat. "Your father has been searching for you. You should head inside."

"But—"

"We will take care of him," he assured her. "We are trained to heal both humans and shifters."

"I ... of course." She nodded at him, then turned to the Dragon Guard, but he refused to meet her gaze. *Fine then.* He could rot for all she cared.

Turning on her heel, she marched back into the house. But her opulent home didn't give her any comfort. Inside, the silence punctuated the pounding of her heart. Was he really going to be fine? Were his wounds healing properly? What if his injuries were too serious? The fact that he needed her help to get to the manor was not reassuring.

Forget him, Vera.

He was a gruff, boorish oaf who called her nag. And to think she was trying to help him!

See, I told you, Vera. That's what you get for being nice.

"Miss?"

The small voice startled her. "Lisbet? What are you doing out here? I told you to go to the basement."

"But, miss ..." Wide blue eyes blinked at her. "The dragon ... is he hurt?"

"Yes," she said. "But he will be all right. The nurses are helping him." Swallowing the lump in her throat, she led the child toward the basement shelter. Before they turned the corner, she looked back at the door, a knot in her chest growing.

He's a dragon, she told herself. He's going to be fine.

What do you care, Vera? You—

NO! Vera screamed at the voice. *Shut up! I'm tired of listening to you.*

"It's so noisy outside," Lisbet said, slipping a hand into hers.

Indeed, in the distance, she heard the sounds of explosions. Her stomach twisted into knots at what could be happening right now. Did everyone have time to take shelter?

She gave Lisbet's hand a squeeze. "Everything will be all right. Now come, let's go somewhere safe."

CHAPTER 1

Present time ...

"**...A**nd I'm very thankful to have you here for this event and for your support of the Children's Foundation. Because of your generosity, we will be able to keep our doors open to those who need it most. You all deserve a round of applause." Queen Sybil paused her speech to let the audience applaud. "Thank you for allowing me to ramble on. Now, please, enjoy your lunch," she concluded to the board members of the Queen's Trust, major donors, and their guests, who all clapped once more and stood up as Her Majesty left the podium.

Vera caught Queen Sybil's eye as she climbed down the steps of the dais. "That was an amazing speech, Your Majesty."

"I have my staff to thank for that," Queen Sybil chuckled. "Thank you again for all your hard work organizing this luncheon, Vera."

"Of course, Your Majesty, my pleasure."

"I can always count on you, and I know the Children's Foundation is so close to your heart." Queen Sybil linked arms with her. "Now, let's go eat! I'm starving!" She placed a hand over her large belly. "We both are."

"I'm sure you are." Vera ignored the pang of envy growing in her chest. Queen Sybil, after all, had become her dearest friend in the last three years and she would never begrudge her any happiness.

I just wish I could have what she had.

A family of her own.

But maybe, she thought, *just maybe, that might happen soon.* Her stomach was a bundle of nerves at the excitement—and terror—at the steps she took weeks ago to make that dream come true. It had taken all her courage, but she finally did it.

"So," Queen Sybil began, lowering her voice. "I see that Jarl Armundson is seated next to you. Again." She nodded at their table in the center of the room, where the other VIPs were seated. Indeed, on the seat next to the one Vera was to occupy was the young jarl. "That's what ... the third time this month? He does seem to like these boring events a great deal." She lifted a dark brow and nudged her with her elbow. "Unless he's interested in something—or someone —else?"

"Oh please, could you be more obvious, Your Majesty?" Vera teased back, trying to shift the subject. "Tobi is an old friend of the family. He lives in London most of the year, but since his father died a few months ago and he inherited the jarldom, he's decided to settle back in the Northern Isles."

"And settle down, maybe?"

Vera grew quiet, not sure what to tell her friend, because

she didn't want to lie. She just wasn't ready to discuss *that* with Queen Sybil yet.

Thank goodness they had arrived at the table before the queen could ask any more questions. All the other guests stood up as the queen took her place, as did Vera on her left. With a nod, Her Majesty sat down, and the other guests followed suit.

"Vera, I know I've said it a million times today, but you look beautiful," Tobi remarked as she settled into her chair.

"Thank you. And I know I haven't said it at all, but you look very nice too." Of course, that was an understatement. Tall, blond, and athletic, Jarl Tobias Armundson was nothing short of a dreamy Prince Charming, especially in his dark, tailored Armani suit. His easy smile and sparkling blue eyes drew people in and she'd seen him in many a website and magazine list of top eligible bachelors in Europe.

"You are too kind," he replied. "And this event is superb. Your hard work truly paid off."

"I'm only happy to perform my duty as head of the organizing committee. And really, the staff did most of the difficult tasks."

"You are not only gorgeous, but also talented and humble." Tobi raised his wineglass toward her. "I wanted to let you know how much I enjoyed our dinner the other night."

Vera reached for her glass and took a sip. "Mm-hmm."

"And I was wondering"—he leaned in closer—"if you had thought about my question more since then?"

"Mm-hmm."

The smile on his lips didn't quite reach his eyes. "That's not really an answer, is it?"

Vera swallowed the water. Hard. "Tobi ... I need time."

"Of course. I'm here if you have any more questions or concerns." He leaned back in his chair. "It's a big decision."

Big didn't even describe it.

Because how did one respond to a marriage proposal that seemingly came out of nowhere?

Thankfully, the luncheon service began. Vera felt a headache coming on and put her water glass down. As she watched the servers place hot rolls and pats of seashell-shaped butter on the plates, she contemplated Tobi's words from that night.

The Armundsons and Solveigsons had been friendly for generations and she actually grew up around Tobi and his family. He was a few years older than her, so after he left for school abroad, she hadn't seen much of him, except for a few gatherings here and there.

But since he moved back to the Northern Isles a few months ago, they'd bumped into each other frequently at events like today. Recently, they'd gone out to dinner several times, usually with her father but also by themselves. There was light flirting between them, but they hadn't spoken of any kind of exclusive arrangement, which was why his proposal the other night had caught her off guard.

"I think it's time I told you of my true intentions," he had said as they finished their meal at La Niche, one of the best restaurants in Odelia. "It seems obvious to me that a union between our two families would be advantageous."

Vera had nearly choked on her dessert. "I beg your pardon?"

"Vera," he had said, taking her hand. "I admire and like you very much. And you wouldn't have agreed to spend time with me the past couple of weeks if you didn't feel the same way, right?"

She supposed he wasn't wrong. "I ... of course."

"Then you must agree that we are compatible, in every way. Both in status and our mutual interests."

"Are you saying what I think you're saying?" She didn't want to even hear it aloud.

"Yes. I think you and I should get married."

It wasn't exactly the proposal she'd dreamt of. "I ... I don't know what to say. We hardly know each other."

"We've known each other since we were children," he pointed out. "But you don't have to say yes now. I understand that this may have come out of the blue, but I've always had feelings for you."

Now, *that* took her aback. "Y-you do? You never mentioned it before."

"You were much too young for me when I left for London," he explained. "I didn't even think of you in that way."

"I see."

"Perhaps I'm being too forward right now, and I don't mean to come on strong. I'm not one to play games, and commitment is what I'm seeking with my proposal." When she remained silent, he continued. "Perhaps we could spend more time getting to know each other? Then you can make your decision."

What was she supposed to have said? That sounded reasonable enough. "I ... of course."

And so, here she was again with him, except this time, it was a public event. She'd been so busy the past couple of days, prepping for this event and her upcoming trip to Paris, that she hadn't thought anything of it when Tobi suggested he pick her up in his car so they could ride to the Grand Odelia Hotel together where the event was being held. But when they arrived at the event and sat next to each other, it was an obvious signal to their peers that they were "together."

It's not that she was opposed to the idea of marriage. Indeed, for a while, it was all she ever thought of. It made her cringe, thinking of her antics in the past, trying to bag the then-Prince Aleksei. In her mind, their pairing had made sense.

But in the last three years, her idea of marriage and a husband had completely changed. And she had other priorities she wanted to pursue.

"Lady Vera! Lady Vera!"

Vera's mood lifted as soon she heard the familiar young voice. "Lisbet," she greeted warmly as the girl ran up to their table. "You were so excellent during the program." Whenever there was an event for the Children's Foundation, Vera always made sure to include the children. After all, they were the main reason they were here, and it was good for the board members and trustees to see where their money was going to.

Initially, the Children's Foundation had been the main orphanage in the Northern Isles, caring for children who'd lost their parents or been abandoned. Since their population wasn't that large, the original orphanage hadn't been that big. But after the attack on the Northern Isles three years ago and the amount of lives lost when the drones had reached the cities, many children had been orphaned. With the help of the new queen, a new foundation had been born, and Vera had been one of the first to volunteer.

"I practiced my singing for a whole month," Lisbet said

proudly. Her eyes darted toward Tobi, her expression turning curious.

"And who's this lovely young thing?" he asked.

Vera wrung her hands in her lap. "Tobi, this is Lisbet. Lisbet, meet Jarl Tobias Armundson."

Lisbet executed a perfect little curtsey. "Nice to meet you, my lord."

"Charming," Tobi commented. "What is she doing here? Shouldn't she be with the other children?" He cocked his head to the other side of the room, where all the other kids were seated.

"Lisbet knows she can always come to me," Vera proclaimed in a chilly tone.

"Of course," Tobi said apologetically. "I just thought ... she shouldn't miss her lunch."

Vera stood up. "You're right, I should see that she get some food." Taking the child's hand, she gently guided Lisbet back to the kids' table. "I really am proud of you, Lisbet," she began. "You've done so well."

"Thank you, Lady Vera," she said. "Mrs. Jacobsen says if I study my lessons really hard and work on being polite and kind, I might find a nice couple to adopt me this year."

Vera's step faltered. *A nice couple to adopt her? But ...*

"That's, er, nice." When they reached the children's table, she led Lisbet back to her seat and greeted the rest of the children, telling them how wonderful they were during the program. Before leaving, she leaned down toward Lisbet. "I'll miss you, *lilla du*."

"Stay safe in Paris," she whispered back. "And don't forget to send me postcards."

"I won't." She smiled down at the girl. "And I'll be back before you know it."

Small arms reached around her neck and hugged her close, and a lump grew in Vera's throat. Finally, they released each other, and she mussed Lisbet's hair before turning on her heel. However, instead of going back to her chair, she marched toward the table where the staff of the Children's Foundation were seated.

Sweat built up in her palms. Vera told herself she would be patient. She had already taken the first step a few weeks ago when she asked to speak privately with the director of the Children's Foundation, Mrs. Lara Jacobsen. The director hadn't been surprised by her request, but had told Vera she needed to look into a few things before giving her a final answer.

"Excuse me, Mrs. Jacobsen?" she said to the older blonde woman in a light-colored pantsuit.

"Lady Vera," Lara Jacobsen greeted. "This has been such a wonderful luncheon. The children truly enjoyed themselves. Thank you so much for having us here."

"Of course, I wouldn't dream of organizing an event without them."

"Before Lady Vera became a member of the Queen's Trust board and started volunteering with us, we were never invited to such hoity-toity events, much less the children," she explained to the rest of the staffers. "Anyway, what can I do for you, my lady?"

"If you wouldn't mind, could I speak to you in private? For just five minutes?"

Mrs. Jacobsen put her napkin on the table. "Of course. Let's head to the ladies' room." She stood up, and they walked out of the ballroom, to the hallway off to the left of the lobby.

"Mrs. Jacobsen, I hope you don't think I'm nagging, but I was wondering if you'd looked into the ... matter I asked you about."

"Oh yes, about that." She slowed her steps until they stopped about halfway. "Actually, I have."

Vera inhaled a quick breath. "And?"

The look on Mrs. Jacobsen's face told Vera it was not the news she had hoped for. "Let me start by saying that personally, I fully support you and am grateful for everything you've done for the Children's Trust. I know you and Lisbet have grown close over the last three years."

Vera could feel the "but" coming up, so she braced herself.

"But ... I'm really sorry, Lady Vera." She let out a sigh. "Our laws are firm. Only a married couple can adopt a child they are not related to."

Though Vera had prepared herself for this news, it still hit her hard hearing it aloud. "And no one has been granted an exception?"

"I'm afraid not since the laws were put in place decades ago," she explained.

"But I can provide her with a good life. A better life with me. Should that not be reason enough?"

Mrs. Jacobsen gave her a sympathetic look. "I know that, my lady. And our laws are so terribly outdated. But they are still the law and were put in place to put a child's best interests first."

Vera bit her lip. "I see ... and if I could hire a solicitor to take my case to the courts?"

"You could try, of course, but it might take a while. Years even. And then that means ... well ... Lisbet might ..."

She knew what Mrs. Jacobsen was too polite to say. "Might lose her chance at having a real family."

Sadness crossed the other woman's face. "I don't blame you for wanting to fight for her, but if she's tied up in a court battle, no potential parents would want to take her in, knowing they'd have to give her up if the courts were to rule against them. It would be too painful for them to give up something they wanted so badly."

Her heart sank, knowing what that pain was like. "I ... understand."

"Lady Vera." Mrs. Jacobsen placed a comforting hand on her arm. "If I may be frank ... you're quite young, still. There's time for you to meet a nice man and have a family of your own. And even if you could adopt Lisbet, no man would want to take care of a burden that wasn't his."

"She's won't be a burden," she snapped, then quickly added, "I'm sorry. My apologies. I don't mean to be rude." And she did want children of her own, but she knew that Lisbet was hers too. Somehow, her heart had chosen this slip of girl the moment she'd laid eyes on her.

"No, I was the one being rude. Forgive me, my lady." She bowed her head low. "I really don't know your other options. You're good friends with the king and queen. Perhaps they could influence parliament to update the laws? But then again, any kind of legislative action would also take years."

That, and she would never think to abuse her relationship with Queen Sybil and King Aleksei in such a manner. But still, there was no stopping her heart from breaking at that very moment. "So there really is no way."

"Well, there is *one* way," Mrs. Jacobsen said. "The law says only a *married* couple could adopt."

A married couple.

Vera's stomach knotted. "I see." She wrung her hands together. "Well ... thank you anyway, Mrs. Jacobsen." Giving the other woman a goodbye nod, she walked away, heading back toward the ballroom.

Where the solution to her problem was waiting.

She halted, shaking her head. No, *that* wasn't the solution. It was the easy way out. Marrying Tobi just so she could adopt Lisbet didn't feel right. It didn't feel fair, not to Tobi or Lisbet.

But then she could get what she wanted.

It also felt selfish and wrong.

Despite wanting to provide a good, loving home for Lisbet, Vera knew she couldn't just marry a man she didn't know just to achieve her goals.

And then there was the fact that she didn't love Tobi.

But did that matter? He's a jarl, rich, and connected. And since when did you care about love?

Perhaps a few years ago, she didn't think such a thing would matter to her. Shame filled her, thinking of how she'd acted growing up, thinking that marriage and a husband was just another accessory she could acquire to make herself superior to others.

Vera, remember what I—

She quickly shut that voice down. Oh, in the last few years she'd gotten better at it, but once in a while, she let her guard down and it still slipped by. Even after Erika Solveigson had died, her "lessons" remained ingrained in Vera's brain, her voice a presence in her mind as she grew up, telling her that she had to get ahead by any means possible.

But that had changed in the last few years.

She had changed.

Right?

Straightening her shoulders, Vera mentally prepared herself to face Tobi and walked back into the ballroom. As she made her way back to her seat and spied Tobi, she wondered, would it be that bad? Couldn't she learn to love him eventually?

From out of nowhere, a prickle came down the back of neck. Like someone was watching her. Following her instinct, she swung her gaze to the west side of the room by one of the exits. She halted, and a different kind of emotion gripped her as she stared back into the familiar steely gaze.

Him.

The eye contact with the Dragon Guard was brief as he continued to scan the room for threats. Yet, she couldn't control the thrill that ran down the back of her knees, making them weaken.

Why did he always have to be around? Well, that was a silly question. He was a Dragon Guard, so of course he had to be with the queen. But why did he always unnerve her with those granite eyes?

And why did she feel lost whenever he wasn't looking at her?

Try as she might, she'd never forget that night when she'd tried to help uncover a traitor who may have been behind the assassination attempt on the king. She'd made a miscalculation and had been compromised. The way he charged in and rescued her made her heart flutter madly, like he was some hero in a fairy tale. Since then, she'd been tongue-tied around him, and her stomach refused to stop flipping when she spied him.

When her knees finally felt like they had returned to normal, she carefully made her way back to her seat. She gave one last glance at the children's section and waved to Lisbet, who flashed her that adorable gap-toothed smile and waved back.

"Everything all right?" Tobi asked as he helped her into her chair.

"Yes." She reached for her water, then changed her mind and picked up her wine glass instead. After a healthy sip, the warmth of the alcohol calmed the nerves she didn't realize were frazzled. "Tobi, about your question ..."

"Yes?"

"I want you to know ... I'm considering it. Seriously."

"You are?" His voiced rose hopefully.

"You're right about a few things. However, I can't give you an answer now, but I think when I come back from Paris in a few weeks, I'll be closer to giving you one."

His Prince Charming smile lit up his face. "That's better than I could hope for." Reaching for her hand, he held it up to his lips and kissed it softly. "I look forward to your answer."

Vera pasted a stiff smile onto her face.

CHAPTER 2

Stein scratched at the stiff collar of the white shirt, cursing Rorik for what seemed like the hundredth time that morning.

Stupid captain. Stupid monkey suit.

When Rorik showed up to his suite this morning with the outfit, he'd immediately refused to wear it.

It makes no sense for me to wear that finery, he had told the captain of the Dragon Guard. *I will wear my normal uniform or even my armor and remain Cloaked for the entire visit.*

"Stein, please." Rorik had pushed the garment bag into his hand not-so-gently. "This is no ordinary visit. You will be traveling to a foreign land, representing our kingdom and King Aleksei himself. You must follow protocol."

If they don't know I am there then there is no protocol to follow.

"That's not how this works," Rorik had reminded him. "What if you are needed to assist in protecting Prince Mikhail and Princess Alyx from the paparazzi? You cannot just materialize in your armor. The world cannot know that we dragons possess special powers aside from shifting into our animals. The Dragon Council will riot."

But—

"Even when I traveled with the king and queen during the royal European tour, I had to wear a suit. You must look and act like a normal bodyguard. Now, come on, just put it on."

No.

"All right then, you leave me no choice. Stein, you are relieved of the Paris assignment. I'll ask Niklas or Gideon to—"

"No!" he growled aloud, then added, *Gideon should concentrate on finding our enemies and a cure for The Wand, while Niklas has young children to care for which means he must stay.* He had grabbed the garment bag with such force, it made a whipping sound. "I will ... wear the suit."

And now, here he was, looking like an idiot in the much too tight suit, waiting at the foot of the stairs leading to the private jet for his assignment to begin.

It was only a two-day trip, he reminded himself. After he delivered those two nitwits to their destinations and ensure the prince and princess were safe, he would leave Paris immediately.

His dragon roared in displeasure.

Quiet!

Looking ahead in the distance, he spied the black SUV approaching the airstrip. The seams of the suit strained against his shoulders as he attempted to shrug. With an annoyed grunt, he stood still as a rock, watching as the SUV arrived and stopped on the tarmac. From the front passenger's side seat, a hulking, bald, and tattooed dragon emerged. Polite, reserved, yet fierce as an ox, Stein thought Ranulf of House Dalgaard an excellent choice for the Dragon Guard. Or at least, he was the lesser of the morons in the recent training pool he'd had the displeasure of leading.

And speaking of morons ...

"Looking good, Stein!" Magnus of House Asgeir, another newly appointed Dragon Guard, crowed as he exited from the right rear passenger side. "You clean up nice."

When Magnus patted him on the shoulder, Stein sent him a death glare. *Just because I am no longer your Weapons Master does not mean I cannot find other ways to make you hurt.*

Magnus merely grinned at him. "Aww, don't be like that."

Once a trainee became a full-fledged member of the Dragon Guard, he was accepted into the fold with equal status among the others. Magnus seemed to have taken that quite literally and acted like Stein was his peer and not his former trainer who had put him through hell the last year.

Did you forget your duties? Stein cocked his head toward the other passenger side door. *Will I have to babysit you during our trip?*

"Wha—oh!" Magnus slapped a hand over his forehead. "Right!" He scrambled to open the door. "Presenting, His Royal Hotness, Prince Mikhail of Zaratena and the Northern Isles!"

"I hope you don't plan to introduce me that way each time we go somewhere," the handsome, dark-haired prince tutted as he alighted from the SUV. However, the smile on his face belied the disapproval in his tone. In fact, when the

Dragon Guard and prince locked eyes, it was as if there was no one else around them.

Stein felt an unhappy grumble from his inner dragon. Straightening his shoulders, he said, "Welcome, Prince Mikhail. If you are unhappy with your security detail, I can—"

"It's all right, we're just joking." Prince Mikhail gave him a nod. "Don't worry, I'll keep an eye out on him."

It is you who should be keeping an eye out on him, Stein scolded Magnus.

"Oh, don't you worry, Stein," Magnus chuckled. "We can't keep our eyes off each other." Then he waggled his eyebrows at the prince.

Ranulf rolled his eyes. "Oh, for the love of Odin. This is our first assignment as Dragon Guards. Can you not act professionally for once?"

"Oh yeah? Well, I'd like to see you act professionally once we see Princess Alyx," Magnus retorted. "Especially since it's been weeks since you've seen your *mate*."

Ranulf turned completely red all the way to the top of his tattooed, bald head.

A twinge plucked at Stein's chest, as it always did when he heard that particular word.

"Alyx will be thrilled to see you, Ranulf," Prince Mikhail commented. "After she's done killing us all for hiding the fact that you've passed the training and are now assigned to her. But she'll be happy."

"Thank you, Your Highness," he replied. "My dragon has been restless and ornery, being away from her all this time."

Stein's own dragon snorted in response, but he reined it in tight. *Stubborn goat.*

"I'm sure it is." Magnus elbowed him. "Stein, maybe you could use a mate too. Get rid of that ... orneriness."

"That word doesn't mean what you think it does, *lubiya*," Prince Mikhail said gently. "But ... ah, here's our second passenger." He nodded to the limousine entering through the gates of the airstrip. "Sorry, forgot to mention, she told me she was delayed this morning."

Stein's heart stuttered, but he ignored it. "Magnus, take His Highness inside and get him settled in. We're already running two minutes late."

"You go ahead, I'll stay here and make sure they load the bags," Ranulf said.

As Magnus and the prince climbed up the stairs, Stein fixed his gaze on the horizon, preparing himself for the inner battle with his dragon. Gods, he should have been used to this by now after six years. But it never got any easier.

"Thank you for not beating Magnus to a bloody pulp," Ranulf said once the couple was gone. "I know he tests your patience frequently, but he's a good guard. He would never let anything happen to the prince."

Though Stein did not track the movements of the limousine with his eyes, he could feel it getting closer.

"I know we have yet to prove it," Ranulf continued. "But I would lay down my life for Alyx, and so would Magnus for Prince Mikhail. Being mates with someone is truly special. It's ..."

The limousine stopped a few feet away from them and the driver stepped out to open the door.

Ranulf scratched the back of his neck. "I know that's vague and you probably can't comprehend it. All I'm trying to say is that you don't have to worry about us failing our first assignment."

He grunted in response, not knowing what to reply to that.

Because how was he supposed to tell the young dragon that he did understand.

The thrum in his veins.

The pulse of his heart.

The call from his soul.

Mine, his dragon roared as the petite figure stepped out of the limousine. As it did the first time he saw her six years ago.

Don't touch.

She's not for the likes of you.

Too good for you.

"Welcome, Lady Vera," Ranulf greeted. "How are you today?"

"I'm well, Ranulf," she said. "I—" She stopped short when her dark violet gaze landed on Stein. And as usual, her bright smile turned into a frown and her nostrils flared in displeasure. "Oh. *You.*" Her eyelids slitted. "What is he doing here?"

The disdain in her voice stabbed Stein's chest like a knife.

"Stein is here to escort us to Paris and ensure we are settled in," Ranulf explained.

"Wait, he's coming with us?" Her plump lips rounded into a perfect O.

"His Majesty insisted as this is our first assignment," Ranulf continued. "But only for one night. He'll be returning with the jet tomorrow."

"I see." Mollified, she tossed her dark mahogany locks

over her shoulder then turned her attention to Ranulf. "Are you excited to see Alyx? I'm sure you've missed her all these weeks. She constantly tells me how she longs to see you."

"I do, my lady, and I look forward to seeing her. Thank you for agreeing to help us surprise her."

"Of course." The sound of her laugh reminded Stein of tinkling bells. "She's one of my dearest friends. I can't wait to see her face when you show up."

"Neither can I." Ranulf offered his hand. "Shall we get you settled in? Prince Mikhail is already on board."

"Thank you, Ranulf." Lady Vera took his hand and began to go up the steps without so much as a backward glance at Stein. His dragon, on the other hand, shrieked in fury at the sight of the other male touching her.

Mine!

Quickly, he turned away. "Get those bags onboard, now," he roared to the ground staff. "We are already behind by five minutes."

As they scrambled about, Stein closed his eyes and took in a calming breath. Not that it helped. He thought by now he would have had greater control over his emotions and his dragon. But it seemed his restraint only slipped over time.

He'd been shocked by the loudness of his dragon's voice when he'd heard it the first time he laid eyes on her and it declared Lady Vera Solveigson as his mate. But back then, she only had eyes for Prince Aleksei. The very idea had him wanting to go against his Dragon Guard training—not to mention, ignoring his friendship with the young prince—and tear the rival male to pieces.

She's not for the likes of you, boy.

That familiar voice in his head crept up unexpectedly. It

had been years since he'd thought about ... that man. He thought he'd put his past behind him.

Don't touch, boy.

She was a highborn lady. A perfect match for Prince Aleksei, their future king. And he was ... nothing. Lowborn scum. Tainted blood.

Too good for a gutter rat like you, boy.

It had been so easy in the past. Lady Vera had been a spoiled brat. Selfish and vain. Treated those she thought beneath her poorly, never gave anyone else a second glance. And everyone knew she was after Prince Aleksei as she continued to scheme to get him alone. And then Queen Sybil came to the Northern Isles, and her vitriol toward the king's fated mate had been plain to see.

"Who the Hel does she think she is?" Lady Vera had fumed. Stein had Cloaked himself and followed her and her father as they walked out of the castle after that first dinner. She had sniped at Sybil all night, trying to unnerve the young woman. "Pappa, what did the king say about this Sybil person?"

"Nothing, dear," he had soothed. "She'll only be here a few days, I'm sure there's nothing to worry about."

"Hmph." She crossed her arms over her chest. "I don't like this. I know something's going on between her and Prince Aleksei. Pappa, you have to do something about this!"

As usual, the jarl did his best to mollify his daughter. "Dear, you're much more beautiful than her, and the prince knows his duty. Even if they had a little ... dalliance, I'm sure it'll just be temporary."

"It better be!"

Yes, it had been so easy in the past to hate her. To tell

himself that he didn't want such a viperous, nasty woman for a mate. He told himself that he hated her and that she couldn't be his, even if he was worthy.

Not after that vow he made long ago, on that day that turned his entire world upside down.

Mine!

He wrangled his dragon away, putting it so deep inside him the silence in his mind jarred his senses. But he had no choice. There was no backing out from that promise he made years ago. And he'd stuck to it too. Never even getting tempted to break his vow.

Until her.

If only she'd remained that spoiled, vile highborn lady. If only he hadn't seen her blossom into this new kind and self-less person who gave up all her free time to care for orphaned children. If only he hadn't witnessed how she put herself in danger to find the traitor trying to assassinate their king. Because then he could continue to deny his dragon. Bury its feelings with hate and tell it that she was not theirs and never would be.

MINE.

Stein massaged the bridge of his nose. There was no use thinking of such things, because even if she did return his feelings, he could never claim her.

Gutter rat.

There were some things that were too broken to be mended.

Dirty delinquent.

The shame of his past, the things he did before he joined the Dragon Guard, those would always be a stain on his soul that he could never erase.

Criminal.

Torture and pain, Stein knew about. He grew up with it, after all. But this experience was starting to show him brand-new definitions of those words.

When Stein found out that Lady Vera would be traveling to Paris, his immediate reaction was to insist that he come along for the trip. He reasoned with Rorik that the two new Dragon Guard would require some hand holding since it was their first assignment. In truth, letting Lady Vera go a few weeks ago to accompany Princess Alyx on her first trip was more than he could bear; it was as if his dragon knew she was out there in the world, unprotected, and it had raged the entire week she was gone.

Coming along to this trip was perhaps the most idiotic decision of his life.

He'd never spent this much time around his mate and in such close quarters too. In the last few years, their interactions had been limited. There had only been two instances he had spent any significant time with her, the first was when the drones attacked and the second was when she volunteered to infiltrate a traitor's home. Both times, he had barely been on time to save her from getting hurt.

But nothing prepared him from being inside a metal tube that was barely bigger than his suite back in the Northern Isles, with his mate only a few feet away. He sat in the last row in the back of the private jet, trying to fix his eyes on a spot and willing himself not to look at his mate or at least, focus on the top of her head. But he could not stop his other senses. Couldn't stop the sweet scent of her perfume from tickling his nose or block his ears from listening to the soft sound of her breathing as she napped.

Thankfully, the flight was only a few hours, and soon, they landed at the private landing strip just outside of Paris. Princess Alyx had been waiting for them outside, but as per the "surprise" plan, only Lady Vera remained visible. Prince Mikhail and Magnus went ahead to the flat to secure it for their visit, while Stein and Ranulf secretly followed the two women around Paris as they went for lunch and took a walk on the Seine. Outdoors, it was easy to ignore the urge to touch her. He was on duty, after all, plus not wanting to intrude on the ladies' privacy, they stayed a good distance away.

Stein did not miss how Ranulf changed being around his mate. His mood was noticeably more excited, and it was as if he could not stop himself from smiling all the damned time.

When they did finally reveal themselves, Stein's torment only continued. He not only had to witness the happy reunion between the princess and the Dragon Guard, but now he was surrounded by two happily mated couples while his own mate was only a few feet away, but still out of his reach.

Don't touch, boy.

His dragon, however, begged to differ.

He'd only touched her once, and he would never forget the feel of her body against his. Even though he'd been half delirious from the pain of his injuries from the drones, it had all been worth it.

Later he thanked the gods for his wounds. Because he had come so close to breaking his vow.

45

Are we done yet? he said to the two dragons. They stood by the entrance of some fancy furniture store, the fourth one they had visited so far. After lunch, they accompanied the two women to shop for furniture, which turned out to be an hours-long affair.

Since the men hadn't eaten since their flight, they all stopped for a quick meal at a nearby cafe. Stein refused to join them and opted to stay outside to secure the area, but that was just an excuse because he didn't want to be once again trapped in an enclosed space with his mate. His dragon fought him the entire time, but he continued to ignore it.

Magnus chuckled. *I'm guessing you've never grown up around any women, Stein.* He nodded at Princess Alyx and Lady Vera as they *oohed* and *aahed* over a couch and some decorative pillow. *I told you you'd find out the true meaning of torture. Those two are champion shoppers. Trust me, I know from being raised by my mother and my aunts.*

How many pillows and lamps does one person need? Ranulf groaned. *And throws. And napkin holders. And decorative bowls.*

Magnus shook his head. *My mother, aunts, and cousins were worse, believe me.* He tsked. *It's some kind of female instinct. This need to decorate and make a space their own. Nesting, some might call it.*

Like female birds? Ranulf paled visibly. *As in ... expecting females?*

This time, Magnus laughed so loudly that several of the patrons in the store glared at them. He sent them an apologetic look. *Dude, you've been wrapping your willy each time you do it, right?*

Ranulf bobbed his head up and down. *Alyx is not ready for dragonlings.*

So don't worry about it. Nesting is just a general term.

General term? Ranulf cocked his head to the side. *For what?*

"Magnus!" Prince Mikhail called. "You must see this footstool. I think it would look great in our apartment back home."

"One sec, Your Hotness." Magnus winked at them. "Ranulf, you'll essentially be living in this flat with her, right? Well, Alyx is doing all this to make you comfortable, too, just like Mik is doing with our new place." Since the two were officially mated, they had decided to live together in the North Tower, where all the Dragon Guard lived. "Mates kinda have this way of making a normal house into a *home.*"

"Magnus!"

"Coming!" He waved at them as he walked away. "Sorry, duty calls."

Ranulf stared after Magnus, then turned his attention back to his mate. "A home ..." he echoed. "I've never had a place of my own."

Never? Stein found himself asking.

"I've always lived with my parents. Then after I left the West Islands, I stayed at the barracks at the Royal Dragon Navy, and then the training center. Never had four walls that was just mine and my mate's." A grin spread across his face.

It made Stein want to punch something.

"All right, we're done!" Princess Alyx declared as she bounded toward them, Lady Vera trailing behind her. "It's time for dinner. I just called my favorite restaurant, and they can squeeze us in last minute. Let's go, it's not too far away."

Fifteen minutes later, they stood outside one of those typical tiny Parisian restaurants that probably only seated twenty people at the most. There was already a line outside, but Alyx sauntered right to the front.

"This place is awesome! They only serve three kinds of chicken, but they're all amazing! Amari!" she greeted the tall, slender dark-skinned man at the door.

"Alyx, *bonsoir*!" He opened his arms and welcomed her with a hug and a kiss on each cheek. "I mean, Your Highness," he said in a whisper. "I have your table ready in the back."

"You're a gem, Amari." She turned to the group. "C'mon, let's go. I'm starving."

Stein straightened his shoulders and positioned himself just to the left of the door. "I shall stay—"

"Nuh-uh!" Princess Alyx shook her head vehemently. "You're coming in too. I booked a table for six."

"It's not appropriate to—"

"Shush!" She held up a hand. "I went to all this trouble to get us this table last minute." Her lower lip stuck out. "Besides, this is my way of apologizing for calling you a booger-headed—"

"There is no need for apologies."

"Stein," she whined. "Do I have to order you to come and sit with us?"

"She's got you there," Magnus interjected. "It's one night. One dinner. Between the three of us, we can protect them from anything. Then, in the morning, you'll be on your way back to the Northern Isles. What could go wrong?"

He blew out an impatient breath. "Fine." In all honesty, he was famished. "But we must do our job first."

"I'll stay out here," Ranulf said. "And you two can secure the room."

Stein and Magnus first entered the restaurant—which was even tinier than he expected. There was really only room for ten people, and everyone sat elbow to elbow as waiters contorted their bodies to wind their way around the crowded tables. However, Amari led them across the room, past a curtained doorway, to a private area in the back. It was not much better than the main dining room, but at least here they had privacy, plus a rear emergency exit.

All clear, he said to Magnus, who nodded in agreement and then left to call the others. They would only have to watch two doors, so Stein staked out a position at the last of the three tables put together. From here, he could see anyone who came in through the curtained doorway.

However, he once again miscalculated once everyone settled inside. Since the two other couples wanted to sit opposite each other, that meant that—

"Oh." Lady Vera's eyes widened as she saw the empty seat across from him. The table was so small if they both leaned in too far, their foreheads would nearly touch.

"I have changed my mind," he declared, backing away from the group. "Someone must be posted outside. I shall—"

"No, no," Princess Alyx insisted. "Stein, sit down."

"I-it's fine," Lady Vera declared. When his head snapped back toward her and their eyes met, a pretty blush stained her cheeks. "Really. There's no need for you to wait outside. You must be starved. You didn't eat on the plane."

How did she know? Had she been observing him? "I—"

"Please." Settling down on the seat, she gestured to the empty chair in front of her. "Sit. Join us."

All other pairs of eyes in the room riveted toward him. Swallowing hard, he did as his mate asked, unable to deny her request.

"All right." Princess Alyx took a seat as Ranulf pushed her chair in. "Let's eat!"

Stein barely looked at the menu and simply pointed to the first item on the list when the server came to his side. And as the evening progressed, his dragon had become even more unmanageable. It ripped at him from the insides, its sharp claws digging into him, urging him to claim their mate. So he remained silent and brooding, fixing his gaze anywhere in the room except for the woman before him. Even when the food arrived, he hardly touched it. Between fighting his dragon and the urge to stare at Lady Vera, he was having a miserable time.

"Are you not enjoying your meal?"

The question from his mate took him off guard, and he had no choice but to pry his gaze away from the emergency exit sign and turn to her. Dark violet eyes stared up at him expectantly.

"It is ... adequate," he answered, spearing a bite of chicken from the mostly-full plate.

"You don't like it?" Princess Alyx asked, her delicate eyebrows furrowing together. "Are you vegetarian? Is there something else you'd like? We can order takeaway—"

"I said it is adequate," he retorted in a rather gruff voice. When Princess Alyx looked visibly taken aback, he knew he had made a mistake. Gods, he'd never been more uncomfortable in his entire life.

Ranulf sent him a glare but didn't say anything, nor did anyone else at the table. That is, except for one person.

"There are children all over the world who are starving," Lady Vera hissed at him. "And here you are, a full plate in front of you, and yet you choose to be a stubborn ox."

Anger bubbled in him. "I know very well what it is like to go hungry, my lady," he said in a low voice. "Real hunger, not because the kitchen was delayed, but because there was no food in the cupboards." His dragon roared at him. Rising to his feet, he murmured an *excuse me*, and stomped out of the room via the emergency exit.

The stench of rotting food in the alley assaulted his nostrils, but he almost preferred it to the stifling tension inside that room. He scrubbed a hand down his face.

"Stein?"

What? he snapped at Magnus as he whirled around.

"You okay there?" An expression of concern crossed his handsome face. "Hey, it's okay. Want to talk about it?"

"Talk?" he huffed. "Talking is useless."

"Is that why you prefer to use mind speak? Because you think talking is useless?"

Stein grumbled. No, that wasn't the reason why. But Magnus would never understand. No one would. "I can talk fine."

The corner of his mouth quirked up. "Yeah? Try practicing more. Who knows, maybe someday you'll learn how to smooth talk and get some ladies to notice you."

"Ladies?" he growled.

"Or gentlemen?" He put his hands up. "I'm not judging. But," he began, leaning forward and raising an eyebrow at him. "You and Lady Vera should either kill each other or sleep together already and put yourselves—and us—out of misery."

His dragon very much liked the latter idea. "I beg your pardon?" *How did Magnus ... did he know ... No! No one could know!* Stepping forward, he crowded the other Dragon Guard against the wall. "I would rather sleep with a poisonous viper than with that selfish, spoiled shrew!"

The sound of breaking porcelain made them both freeze. Slowly, he turned to the source of the crash. His heart sank, and his dragon screamed at him in fury.

Standing by exit was Lady Vera, color slowly draining from her face. By her feet was—or had been—a plate of what looked like a dainty dessert, sitting atop a pile of white and blue porcelain shards. Without a word, she hung her head and slipped back into the building.

Stein smashed a fist into the wall behind Magnus, leaving a large crack.

Fuck.

CHAPTER 3

I will not cry, Vera told herself as she walked back into the restaurant. *I will not cry. I will not cry.* Her fingernails dug into her palms. *And certainly not because of him.*

"So, did the sourpuss like your peace offer—Vera?" Alyx's expression fell. "Vera, what happened?"

Her eyes flickered toward Ranulf. "N-nothing," she sniffed. "Nothing at all."

"You look like you're about to cry." Alyx marched toward her and placed an arm around her shoulders. As she guided Vera back to her seat, the princess and her mate locked eyes. A look of understanding passed between them, and Ranulf discreetly exited the room. Prince Mikhail, thankfully, followed him out.

"Now," she began. "Tell me what happened."

Vera rubbed her eyes with the back of her hands. "It's ... stupid really." With a deep breath, she told Alyx what she had overheard Stein say to Magnus. "See?" She forced out a laugh. "I mean, really? Who said I wanted to sleep with him anyway?" Still, why did her chest hurt whenever she replayed those words in her mind?

I would rather sleep with a poisonous viper than with that selfish, spoiled shrew.

Alyx, on the other hand, turned red. "Asshole! He should be so lucky if you did offer him your V-card!"

"Alyx!"

"Oh, sorry. Right, I need to stop announcing that. Sorry," she said sheepishly. "Don't listen to him, Vera. He doesn't know who you are and what you're truly like. You're not that person you used to be anymore."

"I know." She chewed at her lip. Somedays she even forgot what she'd been like. That she'd overcome her mother's programming, though there were days that she still doubted herself. And then there were days like this when she truly lost faith that she'd turned her life around.

Perhaps that was the worst part. Looking back at all her previous interactions with Stein made her cringe. She had acted like a spoiled brat, bungling fool, or worse—a helpless damsel in distress. Tonight, when he had agreed to sit with her during dinner, she thought maybe he'd changed his mind about her.

But nothing had changed. All this time, his opinion of her hadn't changed. He still saw her as that person she was. "Maybe I still am."

"Still am what?"

"Still am that person. That deep inside, I can't change." Faint laughter rang from a voice somewhere inside her brain. One she hadn't heard in a while. "That I *am* a spoiled, selfish shrew." And maybe it was better that she didn't adopt Lisbet. Who knows what kind of mother she'd be? Gods know, she didn't exactly have the best example growing up.

"Oh, please," Alyx let out a *pfft* sound. "Don't listen to that dickhead. I don't see that at all in you. Vera, what made you change? How did you decide you didn't want to be that person anymore?"

"I ... I never thought about it."

"Maybe you should," Alyx said. "But trust me, you are not spoiled or selfish."

Ranulf clearing his throat made them both look up as he reappeared through the exit. "Alyx, my lady," he began. "How about we take a taxi back to the flat? Magnus and ... the rest of them will follow later."

"Great," Alyx said. "I had a bottle of wine chilling in the fridge for us anyway since this is your first night in Paris. Let's put it to good use."

Vera smiled weakly at her friend. "Sounds like a plan."

Vera turned on her side and let out a long sigh. Glancing behind her, she checked to make sure Alyx didn't wake up. The princess didn't move an inch, snoring softly as she lay beside Vera on the massive king-sized bed.

She smiled to herself. Alyx was such a sweet and dear friend. After they got back to the flat, she insisted that Vera stay in her bedroom for the night so they could drink wine and watch action movies. That also meant that she wouldn't be spending the evening with her mate—the one she'd been away from for weeks, but Alyx insisted that this was her original plan, and it wasn't her fault that Ranulf wanted to surprise her. And the Dragon Guard—gods bless his heart—agreed to leave the ladies alone. Good thing Alyx drank most of the wine, as she passed out cold at midnight, and Vera's tossing and turning did not wake her.

I'd rather sleep with a viper.

Spoiled, selfish shrew.

She huffed and hugged her arms around herself. He'd made it clear all this time that he loathed her via those steely stares and his chilly demeanor. She shouldn't be surprised when he vocalized his opinion. Why should Stein's words bother her?

And why did her chest hurt whenever they rang in her head?

Initially, she'd felt shame at how she had berated him over something trivial like food. She didn't like how rude he'd been to Alyx but she shouldn't have spoken to him like he was a child. Her stomach knotted, imagining what kind of upbringing he had that he went hungry. The Northern Isles were relatively wealthy, but there were pockets of poverty here and there. Maybe he'd been an orphan, like Lisbet. Or had neglectful parents. Or maybe he'd slipped through the cracks. Volunteering at the Children's Foundation and hearing stories from Queen Sybil when she'd been a social worker back in America, she knew there were other ways to abuse children aside from physical violence. That's why she had thought to bring him that dessert, as a way to apologize for her judgement. But then she heard what he *really* thought of her.

Pushing those thoughts out of her head, she glanced

toward the windows. *Morning already,* she thought glumly as she saw the faint light of dawn peeking through the gap between the curtains. Slowly, she got up from the bed. *No use trying to sleep.* She headed toward the ensuite bathroom so she could get ready for the day. *Maybe I should just go home. Alyx would understand and maybe Prince Mikhail could stay instead.* She could spend more time with Lisbet. But then again, if she did go home, that meant she would have to give Tobi her answer.

Had she forgotten about him? It was only two days ago she told him she would consider his proposal. If she said yes, it would only be so she could adopt Lisbet, and that just didn't feel right.

But he wanted something from her too. *He didn't love me, that was for sure.* But he talked about compatibility and status, and Vera knew that language well. Tobi wanted a wife who was equal to him, who would provide him with an heir to the Armundson jarldom and wealth. Joining their two names would make sense, making them both richer and more influential than any other family in the Northern Isles.

It was cold and calculated. Something her dear, departed mother would have approved of, which made Vera reluctant to accept. *But I could give Lisbet a home, not to mention, have children too. A family of my own.* Wasn't that worth marrying Tobi for? And who knows, she could grow to love him too.

Everything she wanted was at her fingertips. All she had to do was say yes.

Then why was it so hard?

With a deep sigh, she pushed the shower curtain away and climbed into the tub. After a quick shower, she put on a light cotton maxi dress and towel-dried her hair as best she could before brushing it out.

The light peeking through the curtains was brighter now, though Alyx remained soundly asleep. As she padded into the living room, her heart stopped when she saw the large hulking figure prone on the couch, but let out a relieved breath when her eyes adjusted and saw Ranulf's sleeping form. There was no sign of anyone else in the living room and she assumed Magnus and Prince Mikhail took the other bedroom. *Stein probably left already*. He did say he was staying only one night. Perhaps the jet was due back in the Northern Isles early today.

Grabbing her purse, she decided to go to a nearby cafe for a croissant and a coffee. As she took her first step outside the flat, a prickle of awareness made her freeze. *Weird*. Shrugging, she shut the door behind her and headed to the cafe at the end of the street. After her quick breakfast, she made her way back toward the apartment, but stopped halfway.

It was a beautiful Parisian summer morning, still quite cool and early enough that the streets were virtually empty, so she decided to go for a longer walk, going in the direction of the Seine.

There truly was no place like Paris. Everywhere she turned, she was greeted by a quaint and pretty cafe or boutique, fashionable women walking in heels, handsome men who flashed her charming smiles. Indeed, the city and its sights would cure any kind of melancholy. Well, almost.

Gods, I have to stop thinking about last night. I—

A loud screech from behind had Vera wincing and covering her ears. *Ah well, Paris was still Paris, it seems*, she thought with a wry smile. Drivers here were insane, and the tiny cobblestoned streets weren't built for the hustle and bustle of a large, cosmopolitan city.

"Hey!" Someone gripped her arm and pulled her back against something hard. "I beg your—mmmmh!" A hand went over her mouth, muffling her cry.

"Hold still, Your Highness!" A harsh voice hissed in her ear. "Martin, get the syringe in my coat pocket!"

"Syringe?" A second man stepped in front of them. He was tall and burly, with frizzy red hair. "That's only for the dragon—ack!"

Vera's eyes widened as the man was lifted into the air, his legs dangling like a rag doll's. The man holding her let out a curse and released her. While she knew she should be running, shock froze her feet to the ground.

"Abomination!" her attacker shouted as he jabbed his hand at the air behind the red-haired man. A familiar shout of agony made Vera's blood curdle, and she watched in horror as a person materialized before her very eyes.

"Stein!" she gasped.

The Dragon Guard released the red-haired man, then reached out toward the other attacker. "You foul—aagghhh-hh!" Stein dropped to his knees. "What-what did you do to me?"

"Vile scum," the man spat. "Martin, grab the princess!"

Princess? *Oh dear*. They thought she was Alyx. Before she could act further, the red-haired man lunged toward her, then scooped her up to carry her over his shoulder.

"Oww!" Vera cried out as she was tossed into the back of a black van.

The door slammed shut with a finality that made her heart slam into her chest. "Let me go!" She banged her palms on the metal door. "I'm not—" She clamped her mouth shut. If they found out she wasn't Alyx, who knows what they would do? *Probably try again until they succeeded.* So, in a split second, she made her decision. She would pretend to be Alyx, to keep her friend safe.

Sinking to her knees, she huddled in the corner of the van and strained to hear what was going on inside.

"... he came out of nowhere!"

"Dragons can turn themselves invisible. I told you it was suspicious that she was out by herself."

"What do we do with him?"

"Bring him in. There was enough Formula X-87 in that shot to keep him down for at least a day. He won't be a danger to us until at least tomorrow, and we'll be at the meeting place by then." He cackled. "I'm sure the boss will be happy that we got the princess *and* a dragon, and we'll be well rewarded."

The door opened again, and the loud thud of Stein's body hitting the floor made Vera start, and she scrambled away lest she be trapped under him.

"Heavy fucker," Martin snarled. "Stay put, Your Highness. And don't try anything funny. Your bodyguard won't be able to protect you." The last thing she saw before the door shut was the man's sick grin.

Vera's brain scrambled to make sense of what happened. They wanted Alyx and they hated shifters.

Oh, gods no!

Those men were sent by or part of the Knights of Aristaeum, sworn enemies of King Aleksei and the shifter world in general. Since Vera had been involved in uncovering the plot to assassinate the king a few months ago, she'd learned more about them. She shuddered involuntarily as she recalled the stories Queen Sybil and the others who had encountered the Knights had told her. Their hatred of shifters knew no bounds, and they didn't care who they hurt to achieve their goals.

A quiet moan pierced her thoughts. *Stein!*

Carefully, she crawled over to him. *Must be some drug strong enough to take down a shifter.* She reached out to touch his bare chest, her fingers nearly recoiling from the blazing hot skin.

"Oh dear." Scooting closer, she leaned down for a closer look. His breathing was quiet, but steady. She moved her hand up the muscled lines of his chest, but his eyes remained closed. *What was he doing here in the first place? Had he been following me?*

He must have done it in his invisible form, like he did yesterday when she and Alyx had been going around Paris on their own. But why? She didn't need protection; she wasn't a member of the royal family.

Warmth crept up her cheeks as she realized her fingers were lazily tracing the lines of ink across his skin. She quickly pushed away from him. Still, he did not move. The darkly tinted windows let some faint light into the van, so she strained to make out his features.

He remained still and deathly peaceful, the craggy lines on his face softening. How she wished for that scowl of his to return to that handsome face.

Wait ... handsome?

Her cheeks were now as fiercely hot as his skin. *Stop ogling him*, she berated herself. *He was hurt because of you.* She backed away from him, toward the farthest corner of the van, then leaned back and wrapped her arms around her knees.

Adrenaline drained from her body, and the sleepless night from before didn't help. Unable to stop herself, she closed her eyes and allowed sleep to take over.

Pitter-patter sounds jolted her awake. The light streaming through the windows was muted, making her disoriented. Squinting at the windows, she found the reason for her confusion. The sky had grown dark and fat droplets of rain began to pound the roof and the sides of the van.

Vera wasn't sure how much time passed, but her muscles were on fire as she tried to move from the position she'd taken since falling asleep. Glancing over at Stein, she saw that he hadn't moved an inch. Fear gripped her heart as she hurried to his side and pressed her hand to his chest. The rise and fall of his breath and the beating of his heart made her sigh with relief.

"*Oomph!*" A bump on the road jostled her particularly hard, and she rocked forward, landing on top of Stein. A breath caught in her throat as her cheek pressed against his solid chest. This close to him, she could smell his masculine scent and feel every muscle in his hard body pressed up against her. A bolt of desire ran straight down her body.

Stop this, you nitwit!

She'd been kidnapped, and all she could think about was how hot and sexy he was without his shirt.

Get ahold of yourself.

Slowly, she slid off him, but allowed one hand to linger on his chest. *Just making sure his heartbeat was steady.* After all, she had no idea what the side effects of that drug they injected him were. However, when she pressed down to feel for his heartbeat, she felt the muscle thump against her palm and a low rumble vibrate from his chest. She gasped in surprise.

Stein's lids opened and his dry, cracked lips parted in a gasp. "My ... lady ..."

CHAPTER 4

Stein was having a wonderful dream. He was surrounded by that delicious scent that haunted his days and nights, some kind of flowery perfume he couldn't name but was carved into his very soul. While he'd dreamt this many times over the last few years, there was a new dimension to this particular fantasy: soft curves pressed up against him and the tickle of soft hair on his nose.

The stabbing pain coming from his side stunned him back to reality. But the sensations didn't fade as he shifted to a waking state. One, two, three seconds passed before she slid away from him, but her hand lingered over where his heart beat madly.

Now *this* was beyond torture.

"My ... lady ..." he rasped.

The hand pulled back. "H-how are you feeling?"

"Like Thor himself stabbed me with a thunderbolt." He winced. "Is still stabbing," he corrected before closing his eyes again. A shiver ran through him as a chill washed over his body.

What in Hel happened? Ignoring the pain, he thought back to the last thing he remembered.

After last night disastrous events, Stein Cloaked himself and ran off before Magnus or Ranulf could berate him. He hadn't meant to hurt Lady Vera, but he couldn't risk them finding out the truth. How was he supposed to know she was standing right there?

Distraught, he had run away but didn't go far. He had headed back to the apartment and waited for the group to return. Once they were safely inside, he had positioned himself outside the building. He'd considered heading to the airport to take the jet back—or even flying all the way back to the Northern Isles in dragon form, but his animal wouldn't let him. No, the ghastly beast fought and raged at him for what he did to their mate. So, Stein stayed, watching over them, not really sure what to do.

To his surprise, the very next morning, the door to the flat opened, and there she was, looking so achingly lovely. He followed her, longing to reach out and touch her and tell her he was sorry. But before he could do that, those bastards came and tried to take her away. Fury pumped through his veins and then ... and then ...

"Those men ... where are we ... why ..." His side throbbed again, pulsing and pumping pain through his veins and another chill passed through him. *Why the hell was it so damned cold?* It was unlike anything he'd felt before. *But where are we now?*

"I'm not sure."

Her answer jolted him to a more lucid state. He must have asked his question aloud. "Why did those men try to kidnap you?" Fury rose through him at the thought that anyone would dare try to hurt his mate.

"They didn't. I mean, they weren't trying to kidnap me." She sniffed. "They were after Alyx. They must have thought I was her. We do have similar hair and we're the same height, so it makes sense."

True. Princess Alyx's existence and her connection to King Aleksei was now public knowledge after all, and the Knights had probably seized this opportunity to take her. And also very likely to use her to gain leverage against the kingdom.

"After they knocked you down, they took us inside this van," she continued. "And we've been driving for hours. They said they were taking us to a meeting place to see their boss."

So, his suspicions were true. But did these men really think they could keep him imprisoned? *Idiots!* All he had to do was shift into his dragon form and he'd rip through the metal like it was tissue paper. Gritting his teeth, he called on his animal and—

Nothing.

No shriek or cry. Not even a whimper.

His body was empty, like a husk. Forcing his eyes open, he looked toward his mate.

Silence.

Dread pooled in his stomach. Then he recalled another detail. That bastard had shot him up with some kind of syringe. *Formula X-87*, he recalled hearing them say. A few months ago, they had discovered that the Knights had invented some kind of medicine that could incapacitate shifters. Gideon and Niklas had experienced it, and they described the pain and not being able to access their dragons. The good news was, if he remembered correctly, the effects were temporary.

"Stein?"

His name on her lips sounded alien. He almost laughed. *She actually knows my name.*

"What are we going to do?"

That was the question. Hopefully, this serum would wear off and he could shift into his dragon and whisk them away. *After I kill these bastards for harming my mate.* But what if it didn't wear off in time?

"We need to escape," he rasped. *But how?*

Before he could even think of an escape plan, the van swerved violently, and muffled shouts came from the front. Lady Vera let out a scream, and he grabbed her and held her to his chest.

As the vehicle swayed from side to side, he used the bulk of his body to shield her as they were knocked about. Preparing for the worst, he braced himself, and sure enough, they propelled forward as the sickening crunch of metal hitting something solid nearly burst his eardrums. Pain ripped across the side of his skull and his entire left side as his body slammed hard against the wall of the van before landing hard on the floor.

Stein waited for the stars before his eyes to fade and his ears to stop ringing before he even attempted to make any move, in this case, take a deep breath. Once he was sure he was alive, he loosened his grip on his mate. The steady rise and fall of her chest told him she was all right for now.

He focused his hearing, limited as it may be without his shifter senses. *Rain. Wind. Thunder in the distance.* Roads must have been slippery and caused the driver to lose control. The impact came from the front, and judging by the force of it, he doubted any human could live through that. *Good*. But now they had to get out of here and find their way back to Paris.

Ignoring the pain, he forced his body to sit up, cradling Lady Vera to him as gently as he could. His shoulder and entire left side felt like it was on fire, and he was pretty sure there was a shard of metal buried somewhere in his lower back. Looking around, he saw the van's rear door had been ripped off its hinges. Gently, he laid his mate on the floor, and with nothing but pure determination, he managed to deliver a swift kick to the door, sending it open.

Thank Thor!

Picking his mate up again, he hauled them outside. Rain pelted him, and the muddy ground squished under his weight, but he kept walking. Squinting through the rain and darkness, he deduced they had crashed along a tree-lined country highway. He trudged toward the other side, crossing the asphalted road and braced himself against a humungous oak tree. Looking up, he sighed in relief as the mighty oak provided enough cover to block most of the rain. He sank down, then pulled his knees up to cradle Lady Vera closer to his chest. Walking through the rain soaked his garment, and now his teeth chattered, but at least they weren't in danger anymore.

Just one minute, he told himself as he closed his eyes. A minute to catch his breath then figure out what to do.

A muffled moan started him, and he loosened his grip on his mate. "My lady? How are you?"

"I'm ... all right," she murmured into his shoulder. "You?"

"I'm f-fine," he said before groaning in pain as she wiggled on top of his lap.

She let out an audible gasp and quickly scrambled off him. "You are not fine! You're hurt!"

"I'm n-not," he said just to be contradictory, but his teeth clacking together from the coldness made him sound pathetic.

"You're lying to me again." She blew out an impatient breath. "And there are no nurses to help you this time."

His heart skipped a beat at the reminder of their encounter from three years ago. They had never spoken of it until now. He didn't even think she remembered.

"It's so dark." She clucked her tongue. "Where in Odin's name are we? I wish I could see your injuries."

"It doesn't matter. They'll heal." *Hopefully.* From what he remembered from Niklas and Gideon's story, the serum not only stopped them from accessing their animals, but also slowed down their healing. *Just need to stay alive long enough for the serum to wear off.* But first ... "We must get out of here and get back to Paris." *Where you'll be safe.*

"How will we ... oh." She clapped her hands together. "I forgot. You can fly. You could carry me on your back, right?"

My dragon would have relished the thought of flying her, he thought glumly. Despite the fact that he'd spent much of the last twenty-four hours fighting with the beast, not sensing his animal filled him with loneliness, not to mention, left him vulnerable. "I'm afraid I cannot."

"Oh." The disappointment in her voice was evident. "I mean, of course, you're not a pack animal. Perhaps I could wait here while you head back and wait—"

"No, you misunderstand." He swallowed to moisten his

throat, which felt dryer than a desert. It had been a while since he'd spoken aloud so much. "I am unable to shift, temporarily. Our attackers injected me with a serum that not only incapacitated me, but also prevents me from shifting for now."

"I wondered why you were so hot—er, I mean, burning with fever." She cleared her throat. "It must be similar to fighting off an infection."

No wonder he was chilled. Still, he ignored it and relaxed his jaw to abate the chattering of his teeth. "The serum's effects will fade once my body has gotten rid of it. But I am fine. And we must leave from here at once."

"It's raining, and we don't know where we are. We should stay put at least until the rain stops." Her eyes flickered nervously across the road to where the van sat eerily still. "Th-those two men might b-be ... incapacitated. And that van's probably wrecked. So we're s-safe, right?"

Dead, most likely, but he didn't say that aloud. "You said they mentioned something about a meeting place and a boss? That means someone's waiting for us and when we don't show up, that boss will figure out something happened and come looking for us. We don't know how close this meeting place is or if they were tracking the van closely. Therefore, we must leave now before their compatriots find us."

She chewed at her bottom lip. "I guess that makes sense. Looks like the rain's slowed down anyway. Where should we go?"

"Anywhere, as long as it's far away from here." He thought for a moment. "The roads around here are well maintained, which means they're used often. They still use above-ground electric lines"—he nodded up at the wooden poles strung with wire—"but the street lights are out. My guess is this storm not only made the roads slippery but knocked out the line somewhere. But that means there should be people living nearby. I bet if we walk in any direction, we could find a house, and then we can call someone."

"But can you walk?"

"Yes," he bristled. Hauling himself upward, he ignored the dizziness threatening to overpower him. Mother Frigga, he hated feeling weak, especially around his mate. The unease made his stomach roil—or perhaps that was the serum—because this meant she was vulnerable and unprotected. *I will fight to my last breath to protect her.*

"Come, my lady." He offered his hand. To his surprise, she didn't hesitate in taking it. The sensation of her soft palm in his rough, calloused one sent a tingle up his arm.

"Th-thank you," she mumbled. "Perhaps ... you should put an arm around my shoulders?"

He wanted nothing more than to pull her close to him, press those soft curves against him, bury his nose in her hair. But he couldn't risk it, so he dropped her hand as if it were a hot brand.

"I told you, I'm fine," he said in a harsh tone. Thank Thor it was dark because he couldn't see her the disdain on her face, though did notice her shoulders droop. "Let's go this way."

He stalked off through the line of trees, leading them to the wide-open field beside the road. Fiery pain punctuated his every step, like hot pokers being driven into his side. Discreetly, he ran a palm over his lower back and found the metal shard buried there, then pulled it out. He gritted his teeth as blood gushed over this fingers. *Pain is good.* It gave him something to think of aside from the fact that he was alone with his mate.

They trudged through the field for what seemed like days to Stein, though in truth, it couldn't have been more than an hour. The rain had stopped some time ago, and so did his shivering. The sky even cleared, revealing a bright full moon.

"Look!" she cried like an excited child. "I see something up ahead!"

He lifted his head and followed to where she was pointing. In the distance was a house of some sort with a steep roof. Grunting, he continued on, focusing all his energy on reaching the house.

As they drew closer, it was obvious this was no home. There were no lights, and the stone structure only had a single window located high up near the roofline, above a large wooden door.

"It's a barn," Lady Vera declared. "A very old one from the looks of it."

"There's no farmhouse nearby."

"Abandoned, then," she deduced. "I'll go check."

"Wait—*fuck*!" he cursed as pain shot up his side when he attempted to reach out to her. *Blasted woman.*

Running ahead of him, she grabbed at the door and pulled at it with all her might. "Oomph!" She stumbled back, but miraculously, managed to budge it open just enough to allow them to pass through. "Let's go in."

The inside of the barn smelled dank and dusty. Light came from one source—a large hole on the roof that allowed a shaft of moonlight inside. But it was dry, and more important, it would shelter them from prying eyes, at least for a couple of hours.

"We can hide here for now," she said, as if reading his mind. "Let me find—Stein!"

A wave of dizziness came over him, sending him staggering forward. She caught him once again, and he grunted as her shoulder hit him in the chest. A loud gasp sounded from her mouth as her hand came around him and landed on the wound on his back. Her breath hitched. "You're bleeding!"

"Woman, I told you I'm f—"

"You stubborn oaf, you are not fine!" There was accusation and frustration in her voice, as well as a hint of something Stein couldn't name. When she sniffed, the oddest sensation thumped in his chest. Was she crying? For him?

"I can walk on my own," he groused.

She ignored him, and her hand gripped his arm tight. "Come on, you lout."

With his strength seeping away, he had no choice but to allow her to lead him away. "Here," she ordered, pushing him down on what felt like a hard bench, then knelt behind him. "Let me see ... oh my ..." The next thing he heard was the sound of fabric ripping.

"What are you doing—ow!" Pain lanced at him as he felt something brush against the wound on his back. "Confound it, woman—"

"Shush, you overgrown buffoon," she hissed. "This is my favorite dress and now I had to rip it up to clean the wound."

"I'll buy you a new one," he said through gritted teeth.

"It's a vintage Alaïa, you can't just buy it anywhere," she retorted. Her fingers curled around his bicep. "Now hold still."

Gritting his teeth, he did as he was told, but it was perhaps one of the most difficult tasks in his life. Because

74

despite his delirious state, his body kept reacting to the gentle touches of her smooth hands. *Thank Thor this place was dark*, he thought as he shifted uncomfortably, trying to relieve the pressure from his erection straining against his zipper.

"I've done the best I can," she declared. "Doesn't look like a deep wound, more like a scratch and it's not bleeding anymore. If you're right about the serum leaving your body then we shouldn't have to worry about an infection. Now, wait here."

He heard the shuffling of her feet, so he turned around.

"There must be something—ah-ha!"

He noticed her gaze was drawn to something hanging from the wall and pulled it down.

"A blanket," she declared, then waved it in the air. "A horse blanket ... it'll have to do."

"Do for what?" he groused.

She spread the blanket on a nearby pile of hay. "Lay down here."

A bead of sweat formed on his forehead, and his entire mouth turned dry. She was standing in a beam of moonlight, illuminating her entire body, which was clearly outlined as the damp cotton of her dress clung to her every curve.

"We both need rest," she said impatiently. "And sleep. Now, go lie down."

"And where will you be sleeping?"

A blush stained her cheeks. "Th-there's only one blanket," she stammered. "But it's big enough for a horse, so there should be plenty of space for both of us."

Every instinct in his body wanted nothing more than to lay beside her. But that would be the biggest mistake he could make right now. "I am fine here," he declared. "I do not need any sleep." The throbbing pain in his side begged to differ, but he couldn't risk it.

She threw her hands up. "Ugh!" Plopping down on the blanket, she crossed her arms over her chest. "I know I'm the last person you would ever want to be with, much less sleep beside, but you need rest so the serum can make its way out of your system quicker. Those men who were after Alyx could be looking for us right now and unfortunately, our best chance of survival is you." She lay down and turned away from him. "If you could contain your loathing and disgust of me for just a few hours, I'd appreciate it. You can go back to hating me once we're safe."

Years ago, during his training to be a Dragon Guard, Thoralf had once hit him with the broadside of his sword so hard, he'd been knocked on his ass and saw stars. This was nothing compared to how her words struck him. It was hard to breathe and his stomach hollowed into a deep pit. Once again, he'd hurt her unintentionally.

It was better this way, he told himself.

She's not for the likes of you, boy.

Yes, nothing could come from acting on his mating instinct. Still, he couldn't stop himself from sitting down on the blanket next to her. Unfortunately, his left side still hurt, so he lay on his back, but that put pressure on the wound. With no other choice, he rolled to his right side, facing his mate's back. Then he noticed her shoulders were shaking.

Fuck.

At first, he thought she'd started crying, but her entire body was trembling. *She was cold*. Freezing, probably. And being human, she could catch a cold or something more serious.

Don't touch, boy.

Reaching behind him, he grabbed the corner of the blanket, scooted closer to her, and wrapped the cloth over them.

She started. "What—"

"Shhh," he urged. "Get some sleep."

He heard her breath catch, as if she wanted to say something, but then her body relaxed. They were so close, almost touching, and he could smell her sweet scent.

Too good for a gutter rat like you, boy.

But something deep inside him roared at the voice, so fierce and loud that it drowned it out.

Then, peace settled over him, and he closed his eyes.

CHAPTER 5

The last thing Vera could remember before passing out from hunger and fatigue was the damp, biting cold that had seeped into her very bones. But for some reason, she was very warm at the moment. In fact, it was very hot.

Oh dear, I have a fever.

But she didn't feel sick at all. No, the warmth was coming from somewhere behind her, like she'd slept too close to the heater.

"No ... please ..."

The rough, gravelly voice made her jolt upright, and her brain began to defog.

"Stop ... hurting me ..."

Coldness gripped her as she slowly turned to the source of the sound. Beside her, Stein lay on his back on the blanket, his limbs shaking stiffly as he fought sleep paralysis, his jaw tight.

"Make him ... stop ... Mamma ..."

Vera's throat burned as she watched Stein suffer through

the nightmare. What should I do? It was bad to wake up someone in the middle of a dream, right? *No, that was sleep-walking*. But she had to do something, so she extended her hand and touched his cool cheek. "Stein, wake—oh!"

She barely had time to blink before she found herself on her back, wrists held over her head, and a massive weight pressing her down into the blanket. She turned her head to the side and shut her eyes tight.

"Stop," he growled, the sound making every hair on her body stand on end. "You can't hurt me anymore!" He heaved so deeply she could feel the warmth of his breath on her cheek.

"Stein, wake up," she sobbed. "Please."

The grip on her wrists loosened, but the weight atop her remained. As she drew her hands lower, she slowly opened her lids. Crazed steely gray eyes pinned her down, as he breathed heavily through gnashed teeth.

She should have been scared out of her wits, but for some reason, only sadness gripped her chest. "It was just a dream." Her hands reached out and touched the sides of his face as gently as she could. "Come back to me."

His jaw slackened, and sanity returned to his gaze, softening the steel into a calm gray.

Thank the gods. "Stein, I—" She gasped when he turned his head and pressed his lips to her palm. "Ohhhh ..." Such a gentle gesture, but her entire body turned to jelly. This was wrong, but she couldn't stop herself as her other hand snaked up the back of his neck and brought his head down to hers.

They both tensed as their lips touched, as if neither had expected it. *Oh dear, I've made a mistake*, was her first thought when he didn't kiss her back. *He doesn't want this.*

However, when she attempted to move her head to the side, a hand cupped her jaw to keep her still. She took in a breath before his mouth sought hers again.

This time, the kiss was rough, his lips moving over hers wildly, devouring her mouth whole. His tongue plunged into her mouth with no warning and his bristly beard scratched at her skin. The sensation sent a shock of heat all the way to her core, and she found herself spreading her knees to let him settle between them. He groaned into her mouth when the substantial bulge under his pants brushed at her hips.

"Yes," she urged as he captured her lips again with his wild kisses. While she always thought she preferred tender kisses, some secret part of her was telling her that this was what she really wanted. Somehow, she knew this was exactly how he would be with her. Plundering. Demanding. Taking. And she needed all of it.

He invaded her lips again, and this time, she gave as good as she got. She tangled her tongue with his, dueling just as fiercely as him. A low growl rumbled from somewhere deep in his chest, and to her surprise, she snarled back then raked her fingernails down his arms. He responded by pushing his hips against her, his erection cradling so perfectly between her thighs that when the ridge of his erection brushed against her, her body tingled with the promise of pleasure.

"Stein, oh!" His lips trailed kisses down her jaw, to her neck. He stopped to press his nose just below her ear and took a deep breath. The rattling from his chest made her shiver from head to toe.

His mouth continued its path lower, moving to the deep V of her neckline, pausing for a second before nuzzling at her cleavage. The cloth of her dress brushed abrasively against the hard points of her nipples, and she had an urge to have his mouth on them. Impatiently, she pulled down the straps of her dress to expose her aching breasts.

Another primal sound rumbled reverberated from him as his lips closed around her nipple. She cried out as his hips ground into her harder, and she wrapped her legs around his waist, urging him closer and hating the layers between them. Her core grew slippery, her clit throbbing as the motions pushed her closer and closer to the edge. Her fingers dug into his massive shoulders as his hips continued to move in a maddening rhythm that drew more pleasure with each stroke. Shoving her skirt to her waist, his hands slipped under her and grabbed her buttocks, squeezing them upwards as he rubbed his erection against her damp panties.

"Stein, please, I—" His mouth covered hers, muffling her scream as her body shuddered with orgasm. He sped up his strokes, his motions pushing her again closer to the edge. A few heartbeats later, he let out a strangled cry, his back going stiff as he surged forward. She gasped as she watched his face twist before he collapsed on top of her. Her body tingled, relishing in the idea that she was responsible for his pleasure. With a soft sigh, she pressed her lips to his neck.

Cold air replaced heat as he unceremoniously drew away from her. Disappointment filled her, but the fierce scowl on his face made her pause. "What is it?"

"He's here." In a flash, he was on his feet.

The haze of lust rushed out of her body, fear taking its place. Her fingers shook as she righted herself and scrambled to get up. "How did they find us?"

He shook his head. "No, not them."

A scream ripped from her throat as a loud crash announced the barn door splintering into a thousand pieces. Stein covered her with his body and sent them diving back into the blanket.

"Idiot!" Stein thundered as he shot up and turned to face their attackers.

Vera lifted her head and gasped. A dragon with light blue scales stood in the doorway, its enormous head shaking off debris. Slowly, the creature began to shrink.

"Did your brain rot once you joined the Dragon Guard?" Stein marched over to Magnus. "What were you thinking, crashing in here? What part of 'wait' do you not understand?"

"I thought you were in danger," Magnus retorted. "Those Knights don't mess around." He glanced around Stein. "My lady? Are you all right? Unhurt?"

She nodded. "Y-yes, I'm fine. But how did you find us?"

"It's a long story," he said. "We should probably get you back to Paris as soon as possible."

"Is Alyx all right? Safe?"

"Yes, my lady. In fact, we've moved to an estate just outside the city temporarily until we figure out what to do." Magnus turned to Stein. "Should I carry Lady Vera or do you want to do it?"

"I'll fly by myself," he replied. "You should take her."

Disappointment tugged at her chest. "You can shift into your dragon form now?"

"Just barely," he said, avoiding her gaze. "It would be best if you ride with Magnus, just in case."

That logical explanation mollified her somewhat. "Of course."

"I've taken Mikhail on lots of dragon rides," Magnus assured her. "You'll be safe with me, my lady."

"I've never been flying." She glanced back at Stein, who seemed to find a spot on the wall riveting.

I wish my first time was with him.

It only took two seconds for the double meaning of her words to settle in, and a rush of embarrassment and heat came over her. The excitement of Magnus's arrival and the relief from knowing they were safe had her lust and passion taking the backseat. But now, it all came rushing back. Steins lips and touch was like a brand on her body, one she didn't want to fade away.

"I need extra space to shift and take off," Magnus said, breaking into her scandalous thoughts. "Let's head outside then we can be on our way."

Flying in the arms of a dragon was both thrilling and terrifying, but Vera trusted Magnus when he said she was safe with him. Still, trying not to look down and hold her composure took a lot of effort, for which she was glad because then she didn't have to think about what had happened between her and Stein. She didn't see him through their brief half hour flight, but that was probably due to her closing her eyes most of the time.

Vera's stomach flipped up like a pancake being tossed from the pan as they began to descend. They were definitely not in the city because instead of the quaint Parisian rooftops and narrow cobblestone streets, fields of green stretched for miles below them. Up ahead, there was a magnificent home sitting on top of a lush green hill. The dragon slowed down and Vera found herself being lowered gently onto the cool, soft grass just a few feet from the driveway leading up to the mansion.

"We're here," Magnus announced as he materialized behind her.

"Where are we?" She glanced around, trying to look for something—anything—familiar. Before he could answer, the front door of the mansion burst open, and Alyx came flying out, Ranulf close behind her.

"Vera!"

"Alyx! I—oomph!" Something warm and soft covered her head. "What in the world?"

"Oops! Sorry." The smothering object was immediately whipped away. "It's a blanket. I brought a blanket. That's what they do on TV, right? When they rescue the victims of kidnapping? Your body gets cold and you need blankets, so I grabbed the first one I could find. Sorry it smells like dogs. I think it belongs to Charles's spaniels and—"

"Alyx." She gripped the other woman's arms and shook her gently. "Slow down. Breathe ... that's it."

Alyx took in a deep breath, but her eyes filled her tears. "I thought I'd never see you again." Arms wrapped around her, squeezing her tight. "I'm so sorry, Vera. They thought I was you, right?"

"It's all right ... shhh ... don't cry."

"I should be the one comforting you," Alyx hiccupped. "After the hell you've been through."

She frowned at the princess. "What's wrong? Alyx? Why are you crying?"

Before she could answer, a rush of air blew over them,

and a tingly feeling ran over Vera's arms. Sure enough, a humungous dragon landed on the lawn, its blue and black scales on its scarred body gleaming in the early morning sunlight. She'd last seen this dragon three years ago, but she'd never forget it. The sight of it made the oxygen rush out from her lungs. When the creature shrunk down to its male form, however, every nerve ending on her body lit up.

"You okay, Vera?" Alyx cocked her head to the side, her eyes scrutinizing.

"Yeah, I'm fine." She cleared her throat. "What do we do now? Where are we?"

Her friend looped an arm through hers. "We'll explain everything. King Aleksei wants to talk to you guys, and we'll patch him in via video chat. C'mon."

Vera allowed Alyx to lead her up the marble steps and through the doors of the classic French manor home. The interior of the place was breathtaking and sumptuous with hardwood floors, Persian carpets, and various art pieces on the walls. *Was that a Monet?* She concentrated on admiring her surroundings because she so desperately wanted to check behind her and look at Stein. Of course, she knew he was there. She could practically feel the vibrations of his footsteps and the force of his stare boring a hole in the back of her head.

"Charles said we can use his private office," Alyx explained as they entered into one of the rooms down one of the main hallways.

"This is Monsieur Laurent's home?" Charles Laurent was a famous fashion designer and the reason Alyx was living in Paris. After designing her ballgown for the Chaillot ball a few weeks ago, he had asked her to be his muse.

"Yes, but he's in Shanghai now for Fashion Week, so he said we can stay as long as we need to. It's out of the way and security's top notch." Alyx led her to a plush sofa in the middle of the room. The three dragons filed in behind them, and Magnus headed to the large TV on the wall then switched it on.

"Lady Vera, Stein," King Aleksei looked visibly relieved as his face filled the screen. "Thank the gods you are both safe."

"Thank you, Your Majesty," she replied. "But how did you find us?"

"We'll explain that, but first, if you don't mind, tell us what happened."

"Of course." She took a deep breath and recounted the events of yesterday. "And then we decided staying in the barn was best until Stein could recover, and this morning Magnus found us."

"I see." The king scratched at his chin. "Magnus, if you please."

The Dragon Guard nodded. "Initially, we didn't think anything of it when you left early, Lady Vera," he said. "We just figured you were still upset from the night before and just needed some time to yourself." He side-eyed Stein, but he remained stone-faced. "When the pilot called us and asked where Stein was, we knew something was wrong. We called Rorik and His Majesty right away."

"Gideon was able to find CCTV footage of the kidnapping from one of the shops where it happened," the king explained. "It took a while, but we were able to trace the van back to a shell company connected to the Knights."

"The van had a digital tracker," Magnus continued.

"Again, Gideon was able to hack it and we followed it. Found the wreck early this morning, and I flew around the area, screaming for Stein through our mental link until he answered back, then I burst into that barn."

Mortification filled Vera. Had Magnus been five seconds earlier ... *that's probably why he stopped ... stopped doing what he was doing.* Seeking confirmation, she attempted to catch his eye, but he kept his gaze on the screen. Her insides wilted at his complete indifference.

"Stein, Lady Vera said your dragon was completely gone?" King Aleksei asked. "Are you sure that's what happened?"

"Yes, Your Majesty."

"Curious." King Aleksei's ocean-blue eyes narrowed. "According to Gideon and Niklas, they could still use the mind link and feel their dragons, but not access it to shift or heal quickly. And you're saying you were completely devoid of your animal?"

"Only temporarily," he clarified. "I am back to normal now."

"Why is that important, Your Majesty?" Ranulf asked.

"Well, it's quite disturbing," the king replied. "What else do you remember, Stein?"

His dark eyebrows furrowed. "They called the serum Formula X-87."

"Just as I thought," King Aleksei tsked. "Gideon said the formula he was given was X-82."

"They've been working on that anti-shifter serum," Magnus interjected, his tone grim. "Improving it."

"Getting it closer to mimic the effects of The Wand." The king sighed. "I'm glad you both are safe. Alyx, I'm sorry about having to take you away from your flat and your work. I promise, we'll find a way to keep you safe."

"Thank you, Your Majesty," she said. "I'm just glad nothing happened to Vera and Stein. This is all my fault." Tears welled in her eyes. "If I didn't—"

"It's not, Alyx, truly." Vera wrapped an arm around her shoulder. "I don't blame you."

King Aleksei cleared his throat. "You must be tired and hungry, Lady Vera. Alyx, can you please make sure she gets food and some proper rest? I have some business to discuss with Stein and the others."

"Of course, come on, Vera." She tugged at Vera's hand. "I'll show you to your room, then I'll have the cook whip up a fabulous breakfast for you."

She couldn't protest as Alyx began to drag her toward the door. Before they left, however, she took one last glance at Stein, who didn't so much as give her a nod goodbye. Her heart sank, but she managed to hold her head high as they walked out. She allowed Alyx to lead her upstairs, not even bothering to admire the beautiful surroundings nor the plush, gorgeous room she'd been assigned to.

Alyx spoke as soon as the door shut behind them. "I really am—"

Vera held a hand up. "I swear, Alyx, if you apologize one more time, I'm going to have to ... to ..." She couldn't find the words, especially when Alyx looked so forlorn. "Come." They sat down at the edge of the four-poster bed. "I'm fine, we're all fine. I hate that you have worry about this, especially since you're starting your career. If King Aleksei can find a way to keep you safe out here, promise me that you won't give up?"

"I promise." She shifted in her seat. "When we figured out that I must have been the target, I felt terrible. I'm just glad you're safe."

"As am I."

"It was a good thing Stein was following you," she said. "I was worried for a minute because I thought if the kidnappers didn't do him in, you would." She chuckled. "And it looks like you two kissed and made up, huh?"

The memory of this morning's passionate encounter made heat rise in Vera, and unfortunately, that warmth turned into a veritable three-alarm fire.

"Hey, what's wrong? You're red as a beet." The air in the room went still as Alyx's jaw dropped. "Vera ..."

"I should go take a shower, I'm filthy." When she shot up from the mattress, Alyx clawed at her arm and brought her back down.

"No," Alyx exclaimed. "No. Freaking. Way."

Vera swallowed hard. "I don't know what—"

"You guys totally kissed. For real!" Alyx tugged at her arm excitedly as she squealed like a child. "You played tonsil hockey! Tongue wrestling."

"Alyx ..."

"Sucked face. Swapped spit. Ran to first base."

Vera buried her face in her hands.

Alyx pushed her hands away. "Vera, I'm not making fun of you. Look at me. I'm just ... surprised."

"So am I," she whispered back. "I don't know what happened, Alyx. I mean, I do. There was an accident and he protected me, but he got hurt. Then we went off to find shelter. We were even arguing most of the way." A nervous chuckle rose up in her throat. "But then we were sleeping, and then he woke me up with a nightmare."

Stop ... hurting me ...

She inhaled a sharp breath. What did that mean?

"This conversation needs food," Alyx declared. "And you need a hot shower." She nodded to the door to their right. "Go on, get cleaned up, and I'll have coffee and croissants here. Then we can talk."

Vera glanced down at her filthy clothes. "That sounds heavenly."

As Alyx suggested, Vera took a long, hot shower in the luxurious spa bathroom. The marble and gold tub looked tempting, but there was no time for a long bath. She did, however, enjoy the expensive soaps and shampoos and the spray of the rainfall shower as the clean, hot water loosened her tense muscles.

Make him ... stop ... Mamma.

The memory of Stein's voice made her heart ache. Had he been having a nightmare? Or reliving childhood memories? Did it have anything to do with what he said the other night about knowing real hunger?

Despite being around him all these years, she didn't really know anything about him.

And frankly, she didn't know if she wanted to. Because what was the use? He had his duty as a Dragon Guard, and she had her own life. Had she forgotten Lisbet? And Tobi's proposal? She hadn't said yes yet, hadn't even thought of him. But the truth of the matter was, legally, he may be her only chance to adopt Lisbet as quickly as possible.

"Vera?" came Alyx's voice from the outside.

She turned the tap shut. "I'm almost done!" After drying

off, she wrapped herself in the thick cotton robe folded on top of the shelf, then padded out to the bedroom. Her senses immediately tuned into the smell of coffee and pastries. "Oh gods, that smells divine."

"All freshly made." Alyx gestured at the tray sitting atop of the mattress. "Come on then, have as much as you want."

She joined her friend, and they sat cross-legged on the bed as they silently ate their breakfast.

"So," Alyx began once the last croissant was gone. "Tell me everything. Did you and Stein really kiss?"

She nodded.

"Was it just kissing?"

Vera hesitated, but shook her head. "There was more than kissing."

"You had sex?"

"No," she squeaked in protest. "N-not quite."

"Did he make you orgasm?"

If this was anyone else but Alyx, Vera would have stormed out or turned to ash in shame. "Yes."

"What are you going to do now? Pretend it never happened or try to kiss him again?"

She took a sip of her cold coffee then placed it back down on the saucer. "Alyx, I honestly have no idea. Oh gods, what a mess."

"Mess? What are you talking about?" Alyx's face was full of concern. "Talk to me, Vera."

"Where do I begin?" She wrung her hands together and told Alyx of her first encounter with Stein, plus their subsequent run-ins. "I've spent all this time hating Stein and for the life of me, I can't even figure out why. Well, I know why: it's because *he* hates me. He acts like he can't stand me most of the time. He even confirmed it the other night at the restaurant. He still thinks I'm that spoiled, selfish person who tried to seduce King Aleksei away from Queen Sybil."

"See, I don't get it either." Alyx tapped her chin, her brows knitting together. Then she froze. "Oh. My. Gods." She grabbed Vera's hands. "He likes you. As in, *likes* you."

"What?" Preposterous. She may be a virgin, but she was mature enough to understand that lust and like could be mutually exclusive. "You can't be serious."

"It's so obvious now. He's been fighting his attraction to you all this time. And he's jealous because of all the attention you paid to Aleksei."

"But he said he would rather sleep with a viper."

"He was trying to deflect," Alyx reasoned. "You know, he was so pissed off when he realized you heard what he said that he punched a hole in the wall the size of Mars. But then he came back and followed you when you left ... oh how didn't I see it? Stein's been so into you this entire time."

"Even if that were true, it doesn't matter." Vera sighed. "Nothing could ever come of it."

Alyx frowned. "Is it because he's a Dragon Guard? And he's not royalty or from a noble family?"

"What?" That never even occurred to her. "Why should that matter? You're mated to a Dragon Guard. It's a position of honor." She shook her head. "No, it's not that. It's something else. Something I've been working on." And so, she confessed to Alyx everything about what happened before Paris, about Lisbet, and Tobi's marriage proposal.

"So, you're going to marry that Tobi guy? Just so you can adopt Lisbet?"

"It's not that simple, Alyx," she reasoned. *At least, not*

anymore. Because the more she thought about it, after this morning, being with anyone else but Stein made her uncomfortable. "I couldn't do that to Tobi. Marry him for my own selfish reasons, I mean. I will just have to find another way to adopt Lisbet."

"Talk to the king and queen," Alyx urged. "I'm sure they'll find a way to help you. I can't imagine what it would be like to be orphaned. Lisbet will have a better life with you, I know it. You love her so much, and she loves you." Her voice lowered in a whisper. "What if you had died yesterday, Vera?"

"I told you, stop—"

"I mean, what would happen to Lisbet?"

She sucked in a breath. "I never even thought of that." But she could have. If they had found out she wasn't Alyx, those men might have killed her. *Or I could have died in the accident if Stein hadn't been there to protect me.* She chewed at her lip then curled her fingers into her palms. "I'll find some other way to adopt Lisbet." *Laws and courts be damned.*

"Great!" Alyx clapped her hands together. "But I think you should totally seduce Stein."

"What?" Heat climbed up her neck and into her cheeks. "S-seduce him?"

"Do you want him to be your first?" Alyx asked. "Was it good? Whatever the 'more than kissing' was?"

Gods, her core clenched just thinking of him and what they'd done. If Magnus hadn't arrived, who knows how far they could have gone. *Very far, probably.*

"Hello? Earth to Vera?" Alyx waved a hand at her. "Oooh, boy it was that good, huh? So why not do it? Take him into your bed. Punch your V card already. It's better than this limbo where you two dance around each other, trying to ignore the obvious attraction between you."

"But wouldn't that be awkward? Afterwards, when we have to see each other ... outside the bedroom?"

"You're both adults, right? And—wait, did you think I was suggesting a fling or one night stand?"

"Weren't you?"

"I don't think Stein's the type for that. He really likes you. I mean, if it weren't for the fact that he hasn't claimed you after all these years, I might even think you were his mate."

"True." She'd heard all about the mating bond from Queen Sybil and the other female mates at the palace. According to them, shifters instantly recognize their mate and have the irresistible urge to bond.

A different thought entered her brain. "What if his mate's out there?" A pain pricked at her chest, thinking about Stein with another woman, the one who was the other half of his soul.

"What if she's not?" Alyx countered. "Look, Vera, you obviously want him, and he wants you. Give it a chance, see where it goes. Go back to being selfish and take something you want. You've earned it. Do it because you want him and he wants you. The worst that could happen is that you two decide you're not compatible, and then you'll know for sure. Get it out of your systems."

"I ... I don't know, Alyx." She felt trapped. On one hand, the thought of being with Stein made her all giddy and excited. But on the other, she felt terrified because if it didn't work, she didn't know if she could survive the heartache.

"At the very least, you guys need to hash it out. Talk about what happened like adults."

"I wouldn't even know where to start. He's probably going back to the Northern Isles today."

"Well, actually, before you arrived, His Majesty, Ranulf, my father, and I were chatting. He's going to have Stein stay here for another day and send Niklas and Annika to stay with us before he goes back. That means you only have tonight to speak with him. Strike while the iron is hot."

Vera chewed on the inside of her lip. Could she really do it?

"If you want, I can help you find some time alone so you can talk," Alyx suggested.

"How?"

Alyx winked at her. "Leave it up to me."

CHAPTER 6

The skies above Stein were a pure, cloudless blue and below, lush green fields stretched on for miles. Usually, a good flight and surrounding himself with nature was enough to soothe him and his dragon. But nothing could quell his dragon's vexation. He initially thought it acted cantankerous because it had been locked away by that foul formula. That was partly it, but there was something else. The damned beast had risen from its prison at the exact moment he and Lady Vera had been in each other's arms, and now that his dragon had a taste of her, it would not let him forget.

It roared at him now, fighting for command of their shared body, urging him to go back to the house. Back to their mate. Back in her arms.

He wrested back control, and forced them to take a dive. He shifted back into his human form at the last moment, landing on his feet with a loud thump. He buried his face in his hands and sank down to his knees.

I shouldn't have kissed her. Now that he had, he didn't

have to imagine what it was like. Her lips imprinted on his brain and on his very soul, as well as the feel of her under him. The shudder of her body as he pushed her to orgasm replayed in his mind over and over again, as well as the mind-numbing pleasure he received in return.

That was the biggest mistake of all.

You're above all this, he told himself. *Don't let your sacrifice go to waste. Think of the vow you made long ago.*

He'd stuck to that vow all these years. That promise he made, to stop the cycle. To prevent anyone else from experiencing the abuse he'd suffered. And what his mother had gone through, gods rest her soul.

Stop, please!

Mamma, make him stop hurting me!

He shut those thoughts out of his brain, pushing them into that deep dark room he had created inside of himself to lock away the hurt. The memories were too much, too overwhelming. Some days they got so bad, he woke up in the middle of the night screaming and raging, forgetting that he'd left all that behind. That he was no longer that scared little dragon boy who couldn't shift.

And some days, he wished that his dragon had never manifested. Or that he wasn't a shifter at all. Because that would mean that Jensen of House Kvalheim wasn't his real father.

House Kvalheim was notorious, after all. Generations of degenerates and criminals. Cowards and thieves who refused to serve the kingdom. No one from his house served in the Dragon Guard or even the Dragon Navy. No, the members of House Kvalheim preferred to use their skills for other things. Robbery, extortion, scams, a few had even escaped the

Northern Isles and only the gods knew what they'd been up to abroad.

His father, however, didn't have the balls and brains to achieve anything more than committing a few petty crimes, and raining violence upon anyone he could get his hands on whenever he felt small and insignificant. And Jensen felt that all the time, especially when he couldn't make any money and they had to go hungry. Unfortunately, that meant Stein and his human mother, Alma, took the brunt of his anger a lot.

This is how you learn, he said after a particularly vicious beating that made Stein's jaw ache for a week. He'd been teaching Stein the "tricks of the trade," but he'd been caught by the bartender he'd tried to steal from.

You have to learn to Cloak. You better start shifting soon, or I'll beat that dragon out of you.

Stein's hands fisted at his sides. He remembered all the pain Jensen caused. Of what he did to his mother.

And remember your vow you made that day.

Fifteen was very old for a dragon to shift for the first time. Most shifters felt their animals when they were about two or three years old. But Stein's had remained dormant. If he wasn't the spitting image of Jensen, one would have thought Alma had been unfaithful. As he grew up, Stein always felt he was a shifter. He may not have felt his dragon, but he just knew it was somewhere deep inside him.

It was a hot summer day. Or perhaps a cool spring one. The details grew hazy in his head. All he could remember was holding his mother's very still body as Jensen stood over them, hands bloody and face twisted in rage.

That's when he felt it. Something deep and primal from

the inside ripping out of him, tearing through the tiny, cheap flat his father somehow scammed another landlord to let them stay in. Jensen shifted, too, and the fight had been violent enough to leave scars on them both. He overpowered his father, but before he could deliver that final blow, the Dragon Navy had arrived and pulled them apart.

"I hate you," he had screamed at Jensen as they took him away. "I hate you, and if you ever get out of jail, I'm going to kill you!"

To his surprise, Jensen had smiled at him, though it didn't reach his crazed eyes. "I knew it. I knew you had it in you, boy." He looked almost proud. "Our family line continues."

"No!" he had screamed. It had taken two dragons to hold him back.

Our family line will never continue, he vowed to himself. House of Kvalheim would die with him. That he would never have children to pass on his name or his defective genes.

It was a vow he'd kept, and one he thought that would be easy to do, especially if he stayed away from the opposite sex. After all, abstinence was the only 100 percent effective birth control. He would stay away from women until he died and his House along with him.

It's not like he had any chance for a normal life anyway. Things hadn't improved once his father was sentenced to life imprisonment.

He'd been foisted onto his mother's father who hated Stein and what he was because of how Jensen had murdered their only daughter. His grandfather was a cruel man and would punish him for every little transgression. Stein couldn't say a word in his grandfather's house, or touch anything, or take anything.

Shut up, boy! Not another word from you.

That's not for the likes of you, boy.

Don't touch, boy.

That's too good for a gutter rat like you, boy.

He left and joined the Dragon Navy as soon as he could. Put all his effort to being the best fighter, graduating at the top of his class despite coming from a House with no history and a bad reputation. When the training pool for the Dragon Guard opened up, he pushed himself to the limit to beat the other trainees and took the only spot. It was when he'd been assigned to stand guard at his first official event that everything changed again.

All these years, he'd resisted temptation. Controlled his urges. He thought it was easy. In truth, knowing his mother's side of the family was just as bad as his father's made it easy to keep his vow. Two terrible bloodlines would die with him.

But then he laid eyes on Vera and his dragon declared her as their mate.

Stein almost laughed. Meeting his mate had to have been some kind of cruel joke. And while he hated reliving his past and scrounging around the recesses of his memories, it was necessary to unlock that deep, dark room and remember all the hurt so he could remind himself why he could never claim his mate.

This would all end with him.

Generations of abuse.

Perpetuating the cycle.

Done and finished.

Stein? Stein where are you?

Magnus's voice in his head snapped him back to the present.

I've just finished patrolling the perimeter, he replied.

One of the things they talked about with King Aleksei was that they had to secure the Laurent estate, which was why he volunteered to do a sweep of the area. That, and it gave him an excuse to be anywhere else but the house.

Great, you should come back then, Magnus replied.

No, I will continue to patrol and check the surroundings for intruders.

I can do that, the other dragon said. *You should go back and get some rest.*

I'm fine, he snorted.

You haven't slept or eaten anything, he said. *You should join Ranulf and the others for dinner. Just relax. You don't go back to the Northern Isles until tomorrow, right?*

Yes. So what? Since Stein was supposed to have been back at the palace today, Niklas had volunteered to come to Paris to watch over the prince and princess, and planned to bring his mate, Annika, along. Annika was also a dragon shifter, albeit an air dragon, but that would mean there would be double the number of dragons watching over the royal siblings.

So, come back and have a nice meal. You've earned it, after all you've been through. A large whooshing sound came fast at him from above, then Magnus's human form landed right beside him. "You can go back to being your usual grumpy self once you're back home."

No, he grumbled. *I will patrol until Niklas gets here in the morning.*

"Well then, that means you're leaving Ranulf alone back at the house." Magnus crossed his arms over his chest. "Because I'm not going back."

Stein stood at full height, which was a few good inches over Magnus. *You will return to the mansion and guard the prince and princess.*

"You're not the boss of me, Stein." Magnus poked a finger at his chest. "Not anymore."

You are leaving them vulnerable, you dung-headed twit. Each member of the royal family must have a guard assigned to them, remember? Your mate is unprotected.

"No, *you* are." Magnus smirked at him. "I can stay here all day."

Stein let out a snarl of frustration. Fine. *But you will regret this.* He vowed to knock Magnus during the next training exercises with the other guards.

The Laurent estate wasn't very large, so it took him minutes to reach the home in dragon form. When he arrived, he saw Princess Alyx waiting for him just inside the threshold.

"What are you wearing?" he growled.

The princess twirled around, sending the skirt of her full-length dress swirling around her like a red cloud. "Versace Couture. What are *you* wearing?"

He glanced down at his usual garb of pants and a shirt whenever he was on duty. "My clothes. I mean, why are you dressed like you are going out? There might still be a threat to your life out there. You must stay here where it's safe."

"Duh, I am staying here," she said. "But that doesn't mean that I can't look nice, right? Charles's chef is cooking a delicious feast for all of us." She cocked her head down the hallway. "Let's go."

Stein sighed inwardly as his stomach protested. *I should have stopped by the kitchen for a bite to eat.* As a Dragon

Guard, he was used to watching people eat during state dinners and other official functions, but usually by that time, he'd have had his own meal in preparation. However, he hadn't eaten anything except for a pastry he scarfed down this morning after his meeting with the king. But this was part of his duty, so he followed the princess until they reached the opulent dining room decorated in gold and silver. The large table in the middle was set with fine china, silverware, and fresh flowers sat in round crystal vases.

"Hey, where do you think you're going?" Princess Alyx asked, chasing after him as he strode over to his usual position by the exit.

"I'm guarding you," he replied curtly.

"No, no." The princess shook her head then grabbed his forearm. "Sit down."

What was she going on about? "Excuse me?"

"I ... said ..." She puffed between words as he tugged on his arm. "Take ... a ... seat!"

"Why are you touching my mate?" came Ranulf's soft growl from behind him.

"I am not touching your mate." Stein shook off Princess Alyx's hand from his forearm. "She was attempting to remove me from my position."

She placed her hands on her hips. "So he can sit down and eat."

"I am not hungry," he protested.

Ranulf lifted an eyebrow at him. "Stein, when was the last time you ate? Did you have anything after that croissant in the morning?"

"I am fine." Unfortunately, at that moment, his stomach decided to rumble loudly.

Princess Alyx snickered. "Awww, sounds like poor widdle Stein's tummy is hungee."

"I said, I am—"

"Stein," Ranulf began. "You're looking terribly pale and tired. How are you supposed to do your duty if you're not healthy? How can you even concentrate when it's been over twenty-four hours since your last proper meal? I don't think you even finished your chicken at the restaurant."

"Each member of the royal family must have a Dragon Guard escort each," he stated. "Since Magnus is out patrolling, that means I must guard Prince Mikhail."

"You can guard us from the table," Her Highness said matter-of-factly. "Think of it this way, we'll be at arm's reach if any ninja assassins decide to jump out of the dessert cart."

"I—" His stomach growled again. "Fine." He stalked over to the seat that the princess pointed to then sat down. "Happy?"

"Why, yes, Stein, I am." She flashed Ranulf a smile as he helped her into her seat. "Thank you, babe."

Ranulf settled into the seat beside her. "Anytime."

"Okay, we're almost ready to start," Alyx began. "Just waiting for one more person."

Stein's gaze flickered to the empty seat on his left. Curiously there was one other place setting laid out.

"Oh, here you are Vera."

The blood in his veins quickened at the sound of the name. Slowly, he turned to the doorway and his pulse jumped. There she was, his mate, standing there, looking as lovely as she always did. It didn't matter if she was wearing a ragged, rain-soaked dress or all primped up in a tight-fitting sheath that showed off her shapely calves and—*Mother*

Frigga—her generous cleavage. She would always be the most beautiful woman in the world.

"Good evening," she greeted, as cool as a cucumber. However, Stein did not miss the way her pupils dilated when they briefly landed on him.

"Glad you decided to join us," Princess Alyx said. "Mikhail will be so envious he's missing this meal, but he's the one who wanted a picnic in the moonlight with Magnus while patrolling. Anyway, Chef Marie says she has a veritable feast for us tonight."

"I'm famished," she confessed.

Stein. Ranulf cocked his head subtly toward Vera. *Help her lady with her chair.*

His dragon pierced its nails into his him, urging him to get up. Grumbling, he did and held out the chair, then pushed it in for her. He glanced at the door, wondering if it was too late to escape.

Ranulf's voice boomed in his head again. *If you even think of leaving, I will make you regret it.*

His head whipped back to the other dragon. *You think you can take me, you unseasoned whelp?*

Have you forgotten what you said about Lady Vera the other night? Ranulf's dark gaze turned deadly. *Your words hurt her, which in turn, distressed my mate. And that makes me and my dragon very unhappy. If you leave now, it will only confirm what you said about her.*

"Stein?" Princess Alyx narrowed her gaze at him. "You can sit down now, you know."

Ranulf pointed to his chair. "Yes, please. So we can start."

Stein trudged back to his seat. He told himself he was

doing this because he was hungry. *I'll eat my fill and excuse myself.*

"Oh, here we go." The princess clapped her hands excitedly as one of the household staff came in with a trolley carrying four silver-domed dishes. He put one plate each in front of them.

"*Merci, Pierre,*" she said. "Now, let's eat."

Stein uncovered his dish. "What in Odin's name is this? Where is the food?" There was a smear of red paste on the plate, while flowers and greens were sprinkled all over the surface.

"Stein," Ranulf warned.

Lady Vera placed her napkin over her mouth, trying to hide a grin.

Princess Alyx shot him a grin. "It's the first course."

"*First* course?"

"Why, yes, Stein. Chef Marie prepared a ten-course meal of her most famous dishes."

Ten courses? He glared down at the abomination on his plate. At this rate, he'd need an additional ten courses after that just to feel sated.

"I think it's lovely," Lady Vera said, taking a small spoonful of the red paste and lifting it to her lips. Her small pink tongue darted out and licked it off. "Beet puree. Delicious."

The sight made Stein's cock twitch, and he shifted in his seat. Sweet Freya, this was going to be a long dinner.

As soon as the final course was over, Stein made a motion to get up from his seat. "Thank you for the meal. I should check the doors and windows to ensure they are—"

"What?" Princess Alyx exclaimed. "You can't go yet."

"The dinner is over, of course I must go."

"But the evening isn't over," she said.

"We cannot go anywhere outside the estate," Stein stated. "By order of your cousin the king."

"I know that." She leaned her elbows on the table and folded her hands together. "That's why we're going to the maze."

"The maze? But it will be dark soon." The dinner had taken at least three hours, and the summer sun was now waning.

"There's nothing else to do," she whined. "And the maze is just in the back yard. You have your duty to guard me, right?" She smiled at him sweetly. "So, guard me."

Stein muttered a curse under his breath. *Was he really going to let this diminutive prissy thing boss him around?*

"It's only a quick walk for fresh air," Ranulf said. "Who knows how long she'll be trapped indoors? It could take weeks before we find a secure location in Paris."

"I wouldn't mind a walk," Lady Vera added. "It doesn't have to be a long one."

His gaze riveted to her as soon as she spoke. He had tried his best to avoid looking at her throughout the dinner, but she was like a magnet, drawing him to her with a single word.

"All right." He tossed his napkin on the table. "Let's go."

As Her Highness informed them, the garden maze was right behind the main house. The sun had sunk further down in the west, but the lit torches would ensure they would have plenty of light for their stroll.

"Come on!" Alyx hooked her arm through Vera's. "Let's see if you two can find us! And no using shifter powers!" The two women disappeared into the maze entrance.

Stein crossed his arms over his chest. *Perhaps I can just stay out here.*

"Don't be a spoilsport, Stein." Ranulf patted him on the shoulder. "Come, let's find the ladies before they get lost and we end up searching for them all night."

This was getting ridiculous. He followed Ranulf into the maze anyway. However, since they were alone, he decided to distract himself as they turned the first corner. *What do you think The Knights had planned for Princess Alyx?*

Ranulf's expression turned grave. *Kidnap for ransom? In exchange for the Wand?*

Yes, that was my first guess as well. When the Knights had attacked three years ago, they used an artifact called The Wand of Aristaeum on the former king, Aleksei's father. The Wand removed a shifter's animal from its human body permanently. While they were able to retrieve The Wand and keep it safe, the Knights desperately wanted it back.

What if they try to kidnap her again?

"They can try." Ranulf's tone was as icy as the north wind. "But they'll have to go through me."

They'll know we're prepared this time. He thought for a moment. *But that also means they're desperate.*

"Could be." Ranulf stopped short, then looked around. "So, which way should we go now?"

What?

"I was following you!"

I was following you.

"Great, now we're lost." Ranulf scrubbed a hand over his bald head. "Let's split up, it'll be easier to find the girls and bring them back. I don't know about you, but I'm still hungry after that godsawful meal."

Stein suppressed his smile. *It was tasty. What there was of it.*

"Hey, how about we find the ladies and then raid the larder? I peeked in the kitchen and saw the staff eating a fresh baked ham. It smelled amazing."

Deal.

They went their separate ways, with Ranulf turning left and him turning right. He tuned his shifter ears, listening for unusual sounds until he picked up some rustling and foot-steps. Following the noise, he turned left at the section, then right, and then another left.

"What the—oh."

Stein froze as he nearly collided with Vera at the next turn. His dragon, on the other hand, did flips and leaps at the sound of their mate's voice.

Her dark violet eyes widened. "Where's Ranulf?"

"We split up," he stated. "And Her Highness?"

"Looks like they both had the same idea." She smiled sheepishly. "She thought it would be harder to find us if we separated ways."

"Ah, I see." His heart hammered in his chest as they stood inches from each other. From here, he could smell her sweet perfume. Gods, how he wanted touch her. Taste her. Nuzzle between those breasts again. "It's already dark. I think we should go back to the house. Follow me." Turning on his heel, he strode away from her.

"Wait!" she called. "Stein, I—"

"I know the way." His hands fisted at his sides as it was the only way he could stop himself from reaching out to her and hauling her into his arms.

"No, I mean, slow down! These heels—ack!"

His heightened hearing heard her shoes slip on something, and in an instant, he was in front of her, catching her before she reached the ground. He wrapped his arms around her waist and pulled her up to his chest. His heart pounded like a war drum in the throes of battle.

What are you doing to me, woman?

Her lashes lowered. "What does it look like I'm doing?"

Godsdamn, he said that aloud.

"Is it working?" Her low tone moved over him like a soft caress, sending a tingling sensation across his skin. "Stein," she moaned, moving her hand up to his shoulders.

Odin forgive him, he could only resist so much temptation. He hauled her up higher and brought his head down so he could taste her sensuous mouth again.

She was even more delicious than he remembered. He could compare her to so many things—like freshly-picked berries or the most intoxicating wine on earth—but then the only way he could really describe her mouth was that it was *everything*. Everything he wanted, everything he needed to survive another day on this godsforsaken world.

She moved her hips against him, and once again, his cock hardened at the contact. This morning, he'd gone delirious from the pleasure she drew from him and he hadn't cared about coming in his pants while they rutted together like animals. If that was what spending was like with her, then actually being inside her would surely kill him. And such a death would be worth it.

Her knees climbed his hips, her tight dress rising up to her waist so she could straddle him. He cradled her ass, each globe overflowing in his hands, and pressed her tighter against the ridge of his erection. Gods, he could hold her like this forever, rubbing up against him until he came again.

A loud giggle from somewhere in the maze, followed by a throaty male laugh, made them both freeze. Stein's sanity returned, and he planted her feet back on the ground. She staggered back, her breathing heavy and labored.

He turned away from her. "We must—"

"Are we ever going to talk about what happened this morning?"

His heart leapt into his throat. "There is nothing to talk about."

"*Nothing to talk about?*" she half-shouted in an incredulous tone. "So that's it? What happened this morning—five seconds ago—was nothing? I'm nothing?"

"That's not what I said," he roared, whipping around to face her. "We were caught in the moment. It won't happen again." *It can't happen again.*

Her lips pulled back. "I can't pretend it didn't happen, Stein. That our kiss wasn't the most amazing kiss I've ever experienced or that I wanted you. W-want you still."

Why did she have to make this so difficult? "We can't."

"Why not?" She took a step forward. "It could be so good between us."

Oh, he knew it would be more than good. A lot more. "It's not right."

"Why? Because you're a Dragon Guard?"

"Yes."

"You know that's bullshit." The profanity from her lips jarred him. "There's more, I know it."

Did she suspect what she was to him? "No, there isn't."

"Tell me you hate me then." The way she stood there, with her chin jutting up, unafraid and challenging him made fierce pride well up in him. "Tell me you still think I'm a spoiled brat. Worse than a viper."

He opened his mouth but nothing came out. He tried again. "What do you want from me? Do you want a quick tumble in bed?" His stomach knotted. "A one-night stand to get it out of our systems?"

Her expression softened. "You and I both know that one time could never be enough. And you're too noble to use a woman just for pleasure."

Thor help him, but she was making this difficult. Would nothing sway her from this foolishness?

There was one last card he could play. Something he knew she was desperate for. Freya forgive him, it was the only way to keep his vow. "I cannot give you what you want, Vera."

She crossed her arms under her breasts and cocked a hip. "How do you know what I want?"

"You want children," he stated. He'd seen it in the way she looked at Prince Alric and Queen Sybil's growing belly.

"W-well, yes." Color heightened her cheeks. "Someday soon."

"I do not want them," he stated. "I do not care for them. Any woman who wants to be with me needs to understand that. I will not be coerced or tricked either. Can you accept that?"

Thick silence hung between them as they stood toe-to-toe. He had to admire her, because she didn't move or shrink away. But he could see the play of emotions on her face as she contemplated his words. And as the silence stretched on, he knew he had won.

He pointed behind her. "Take the next left, then two rights, and a left. That should bring you to the exit." And without another word, he stalked deeper into the maze. Away from her.

His dragon raged at him, shredding his insides with its claws. But he ignored it. After all, there was a worse pain inside him now. And it grew as he moved further away from Vera. His mate, who wanted him. Who had offered him a future with her.

No, he could not take what she offered. Because what did he have to give to her in return? Tainted blood, tainted name, tainted children. The only way to cleanse the sins of his family and stop the cycle was for his House to end with him.

The memory of her kiss, the taste of her lips, the feel of her pressed up against him, all those would have to be enough to last him his whole miserable life.

CHAPTER 7

Vera welcomed the numbness spreading over her body as she watched Stein disappear around the corner.

Gods, what did I do?

When Alyx came up with the plan to get her and Stein alone, she just went along with it. Between her kidnapping, near-death experience, and that passionate embrace, her emotions had been a maelstrom. In her confusion, she mistook his lust for something more. Even fantasized what it would be like to be with him, not just in bed, but by his side. To belong to him.

I should have thought this through. Should have made more logical decisions.

Why did she confront him?

Because she needed the answer. Alyx was right, they couldn't just dance around each other forever.

And she got her answer.

'No' was a complete sentence. She shouldn't have asked him to elaborate. It was one thing if he just didn't want her.

Or only wanted her for sex. But to tell her that he didn't want children and despised them, well that made a big difference. Because now more than ever, she wanted to fight for Lisbet, but she would never bring a child into a home where only one parent loved her.

She already knew what that was like.

"Vera?"

She whirled around to find Alyx and Ranulf standing at the end of the hedgerow. Her throat turned dry and scratchy as she tried to answer. Her stance or her poor poker face must have given something away as Alyx rushed to her side. Ranulf, bless his heart, nodded at Vera briefly before turning around and rounding the corner, leaving them to their privacy.

"Oh no," she cried, pulling her into a fierce embrace. "Did he say something to hurt you?"

"Only the truth," she whispered back. "I don't want to talk about it."

"Of course." Alyx released her, then put her hands on her shoulders. "You're a stunning, smart, and wonderful woman. Anyone would be lucky to have you. If that bull-headed numbskull can't see that, then that's on him, not you."

"Th-thank you, Alyx. I'm fine, really. Just … wounded my pride." His rejection still stung, after all, even if it was understandable. "We did speak briefly, and he—we realized we weren't compatible."

Yes, that was it. She couldn't compromise on the children part, especially not when she might have a long and complicated battle for Lisbet ahead. And she couldn't force him to want children, not if he didn't want them. Stein was an adult, and she would never tell him that he might change his mind or, gods forbid, trick him into being with her by pretending she was fine with not having children. Even if Lisbet wasn't in the picture, she could never trap him like that.

"Let's head back to the house," Alyx suggested. "I bet Charles has an amazing cellar. Plus, there might be some more chocolate tarts in the fridge."

Vera forced a smile on her face. "That would be nice."

When Niklas arrived with his mate the next day, Vera knew that Stein was truly gone.

For the next few days, Vera tried her best to act normal and even cheerful, if only for Alyx's sake. Her friend was stressed enough, and she didn't want to add to that, especially since this was an exciting time for her. Initially, Monsieur Laurent was going to announce Alyx's role as his next muse and protege as soon as he was back from Shanghai, but because of security concerns, he agreed to delay it.

The Dragon Guards and King Aleksei came up with a plan to keep Alyx safe. She would rotate between three different apartments around the city, each one rented under layers upon layers of shell companies that would not be traceable to the Northern Isles. Niklas and Annika would stay on for a few more weeks until they settled into their new routine.

"This is so much trouble all for me," Alyx had said. "Maybe I should go back to the Northern Isles with you."

Since there were so many people around Alyx—Niklas, Annika, Mikhail, and Magnus who decided to stay, plus, Ranulf would be by her side, of course—Vera decided to cut her trip short. Aside from that, she was eager to get started on Lisbet's adoption and had already made an appointment to see a few solicitors, plus, she also had to tell her father. Then, she would ask the king and queen for help. That thought made her stomach somersault as that would mean having to go to the palace and possibly running into a certain Dragon Guard.

"Alyx, that's complete nonsense." Vera placed her hand over Alyx's. "This is worth it. And I know His Majesty will defeat the Knights and then you don't have to worry about being a target again. Oh, we're here." The limo stopped on the tarmac where the private jet awaited. "That ride was too quick."

"I know," Alyx cried, giving her a hug. "I'll miss you."

"Me too. But maybe I'll come back with some good news."

"I know you will." The princess sniffed and rubbed at her eyes. "We'll chat every day."

"Of course we will."

The driver opened the door, and the two women alighted. After a round of endless tearful goodbyes, Vera finally boarded and was on her way.

A mixture of emotions filled her as she neared the Northern Isles. For one thing, it would always be her home, and her father and Lisbet were there and she missed them both so. But then again, Stein was there too. How could she possibly face him after what happened in the maze? *Maybe it'll get easier over time.* They barely interacted before Paris, after all, unless they were sniping at each other. And who knows? She'll be so busy with building her life with Lisbet that she won't even notice him.

The next two days were a flurry of activity for Vera. First on her agenda was to inform her father of her plans. She spoke to him during her welcome home dinner that first evening she arrived.

"If that's what you want, I fully support you, dear," he said, pulling her into a warm embrace. "I would welcome any daughter of yours into our family."

Her throat grew thick with tears. How lucky she was that she had him all these years, not only to spoil and indulge her, but love her unconditionally. "Thank you, Pappa. I appreciate it."

Frankly she was worried he'd object, especially since she was his only child and would someday be Countess Solveigson in her own right. She wouldn't be able to pass the title to Lisbet since she wouldn't be her blood daughter, but her father was relatively young and healthy, plus, Vera figured there would enough time for her to marry and have her own children. If not, the title would go to a distant cousin.

The thought of children made her feel glum, so she pushed that aside and concentrated on preparing for her appointments the next day. First stop was the Children's Foundation, where she visited Lisbet, who was overjoyed that she had returned early. She stayed as long as she could, listening to the young girl as she relayed all the events of the last few days.

"I'm glad you're making new friends, Lisbet," she said as they chatted over breakfast. "But this boy Iver sounds like bad news. Next time he pulls your hair, you should report him to your teacher."

"But I'm no tattletale." She stuck her lower lip out.

Vera chuckled. "Of course not. Playground rules."

As they finished up their breakfast, Vera considered telling Lisbet about her plans but decided against it for now because if the adoption didn't push through, then she didn't want her to be disappointed. Once Vera did find a legal loophole, she would ask the girl properly if she would like to be adopted. It only seemed fair after all, and if Lisbet preferred to be placed in a family with two parents, she would understand and forgo the adoption.

After a quick word with Lara Jacobsen and attending to some business at the office, she headed off to her next set of appointments. She interviewed three solicitors, though none had any good news to tell her or even any *new* news.

"I can definitely research further into our adoption laws, Lady Vera," the last solicitor, a Mr. Liam Hartensen, senior partner at Gloss, Davis, Hartensen & Associates told her. "But as far as I know, no single woman or man has ever successfully adopted a child not related to them."

"But that doesn't mean there can't be a first."

"Indeed." Though Mr. Hartensen looked impressed at her determination, his next words did not make her feel better. "But do prepare yourself for ... whatever may come."

She thanked him and then left his office, her heart a little less hopeful. She did still have one option left. Well, she didn't know if the king and queen could do anything for her, but it was worth a try.

Now, I only have to go to the palace and see them. Asking the monarch's help to bend the laws couldn't be done over a phone call, after all.

Vera had gone to the king and queen's home many times over the last three years, sometimes last minute and without any need for an invitation. But the thought of walking in there and possibly running into Stein made her both giddy and want to lose her lunch, as if she wanted to see him *and* not see him at the same time.

Think of Lisbet, she told herself. *Think of bringing her home, tucking her into bed every night, having breakfast with her, bringing her and picking her up from school.*

And with those thoughts in mind, she made the call to the palace. Queen Sybil's secretary said Her Majesty was busy now, but she penciled her in for later that afternoon. Her hand shook as she slipped her phone back into her purse, but Vera congratulated herself on taking this next step.

As she exited the Gloss, Davis, Hartensen & Associates office building, she heard a familiar voice call to her.

"Vera!"

Whirling around, she found herself face-to-face with Tobi Armundson. "T-Tobi," she greeted, surprised. "Fancy running into you here. Do you have a business meeting or … something?"

"No, actually." He shook his head, his golden hair gleaming in the sunlight. "I must confess, I was looking for you. I had heard you had come back from Paris early and went to see you at home. When I asked your butler, Gustav, he said you were having your driver bring you here."

"Ah yes, er, I only arrived yesterday. And my return was unexpected." She flicked off an imaginary piece of lint from her sleeve. "I meant to call you as soon as I could."

Actually, she'd been hoping to avoid him for as long as possible. *I should have told Gustav not to tell anyone I was home.* "But my father missed me, and he wanted me to himself for the evening. You understand, right?"

"Completely." Taking a step forward, he slipped his hand

into hers. "But now that I'm here, how about we go for tea? I'd love to just catch up and talk."

"I'm afraid I was on my way to—" She stopped short before she mentioned the palace.

"Yes?"

She did have a few more hours before her appointment with Queen Sybil, and it didn't make sense to go all the way home just to leave again. "Actually, I barely had any lunch. Just a fruit salad between appointments. Tea would be lovely."

He flashed her a dazzling smile before tucking her hand in his arm. "Your wish is my command. I know a place, just a block from here."

They had only walked a few steps when Vera's instinct told her there was more to this little run in than just a casual tea with a friend. *Oh dear.*

She was already regretting her decision to come with him, because she could guess what he wanted to "catch up and talk" about. However, it was much too late to decline, and soon, Vera found herself seated across Tobi at a lovely little teashop in the city's historic district. Like many of the businesses in the area, it was located in a finely preserved old building, and the inside was decorated tastefully to match the exteriors—classic turn of the century Northern Isles style, but everything was new or at the very least, restored.

"Thank you," she said to the waiter who took their orders as she handed him back their menu.

"I'm glad I found you today, Vera," Tobi began. "And maybe, I was hoping that you had cut your trip to Paris short because you missed me."

"Oh, Tobi." She waved her hand in a flirty manner,

stalling so she could find a diplomatic way to deflect because she hadn't thought of him at all. "You're too much. No, I'm afraid Princess Alyx has decided that she's perfectly capable of being in Paris by herself. And I was happy to help her prove this to her family by leaving her be."

"Ah, I see." He took a sip of water. "And how was Paris?"

That question was part of the small talk before they would move onto, well, the big talk. So, Vera decided to stall as much as she could. "Why, it was wonderful! I much prefer Paris in the fall, but in summer the weather is gorgeous."

On and on she went, describing the beauty of the city, the fashion, the food, the people, and things she did. In fact, she talked so much one would have thought she'd spent months there. Sure, she embellished a lot of it—after all, she had been sequestered at Monsieur Laurent's estate for a majority of the time—but most of it was true. By the time she'd exhausted the topic, the waiter was already refreshing their teapot for the third time.

"Sounds like you had a lovely trip," Tobi said politely.

"Oh dear, I've completely manipulated the conversation, haven't I? And look at the time," she fake-exclaimed. "You must have a busy a day. I'm so sorry for taking up so much of your attention."

"No need to apologize." Reaching across the table, he covered her hand with his. "Actually, I'm so glad you agreed to have tea with me."

Fighting the urge to pull her hand away, she said, "Of course. I always have time for a friend."

His expression faltered for a microsecond. "When we last spoke, you said you'd give me an answer to my question when you returned from Paris."

"I know, but my trip was cut short."

"I was hoping that the distance between us would have helped your decision along. That's why I didn't try to call or message you." He grinned sheepishly. "Made your heart grow fonder, perhaps?"

"Tobi, I—"

"I can't help but think you've already made your decision."

Vera let out a sigh. He was right. And it wasn't fair to put him off, not when her mind was made up, and she had promised him an answer. "I'm sorry, Tobi. I really am. Your proposal made sense. And I am fond of you, and I'm sure it could have grown to be more."

"Is there someone else?"

"No," she said quickly, then added. "Kind of."

She owed him the truth, and besides, if her battle in the courts became public, he would find out anyway. So, she told him about Lisbet and the adoption. "So, you see, I can't accept your proposal, not when I decided that I want Lisbet to be mine. It wouldn't be fair to you—not with the publicity, and certainly, I couldn't ask you to accept a girl you hardly know."

Tobi folded his hands on the table. "That's all? You're declining my proposal because you want to adopt some—er, lovely girl?"

Vera's pause was longer than she'd anticipated. "Yes."

"Oh, darling, I don't mind at all. I love children. I want children. With you."

Those words should have sent her heart soaring into the heavens. But for some reason, her stomach clenched involuntarily. "You do? And Lisbet?"

"Yes. Her included. But you do want our own children, right? Biological ones?"

She nodded, unable to dislodge the lump stuck in her throat.

"Then marrying me makes perfect sense." The corners of his lips curled up. "You and I can adopt Lilly—"

"Lisbet," she corrected.

"Right. Lisbet. And then we can still have our own children after we're married. Just think of it—our heir will be a double Jarl. Jarl of Armundson and Solveigson."

"Or Countess," she added.

"Yes, of course." He scooped up both her hands in his. "So, what do you say, Vera? Will you do me the honor of being your husband?"

Vera stared at him, like the proverbial deer in headlights. "Don't you need some time to think about this? You've only learned of my plans minutes ago."

"I don't need time," he insisted. "I want you to be my wife. And I'll do anything to make that happen."

"I ... Tobi ..."

"Please, Vera. Do I have to get down on one knee?"

"Oh heavens, no." She glanced around as a few people were starting to stare. Her chest tightened, and the walls seemed to close around her. "I need time to process this. And I should speak to my solicitors and my father. H-he'll expect a proper proposal. And your mother, I assume, would want to know, right?"

The mention of their parents seemed to cool his heels. "Of course, how could I ignore tradition? All right." Straightening his shoulders, he released her hands. "I will give you more time to accept. And I do have to take care of some business on my end, plus inform Mother."

"Thank you, Tobi."

They finished up their tea then got up to leave.

"What day should I call on your father this week?"

"Tobi," she warned.

"All right, I'll be patient." As they exited the shop, he guided her with a gentle hand on the small of her back. "You won't make me wait too long?"

"Not too long." She breathed an inward sigh of relief as her limo pulled up to the curb. "Talk to you later, Tobi."

"I'll be looking forward to it."

Vera fidgeted all the way to Helgeskar Palace, home of King Aleksei and the rest of the royal family, unsure what to do now. After all, she'd been mentally preparing for a long legal battle, or perhaps begging the king and queen for their assistance.

But now, the solution to her problem was already here. If she accepted Tobi's proposal, there would be no need to fight or beg, not to mention she was practically guaranteed a win. According to the solicitors, a normal adoption process would take eighteen months maximum, plus, she might be able to gain temporary custody sooner if the courts could be persuaded. And there would be no deception either as Tobi agreed to the adoption.

But why did she hesitate? What was stopping her from saying yes and gaining everything she wanted?

Before she could answer, the limo stopped, indicating they had arrived at the palace. When she entered the business offices of the queen, she was surprised to find Her Majesty was on her way out.

"Vera, there you are." Queen Sybil nodded to her secretary as she closed her office door. "Come, let's head out."

"Out? But I made an official appointment to see you in your office."

"I know." She pressed a hand to her lower back and let out a soft groan. "But I really need to put my feet up. Baby's been playing soccer with my spleen the whole day."

"Wait, aren't you due soon?"

"Not until the end of next month, plus or minus two weeks," the queen answered.

"Still, that's quite close. Shouldn't you be slowing down?"

"But I have so much to do. Besides, I'll grow bored out of my mind, waiting around doing nothing for another couple of weeks. Anyway, when I saw your name pop up in my calendar, I was so relieved. We can conduct our meeting back at the royal apartments while I'm in my pajamas and bunny slippers."

Vera bit her lip. She'd been hoping for a formal meeting to ask the queen's assistance, to keep things legal and above board, should the adoption ever be questioned.

"We can have dinner afterwards, and you can help me tuck Alric in."

The mention of the young crown prince had her perking up. "How can I resist such an offer?"

"Excellent. My escort's here." She waved to Rorik, the Captain of the Dragon Guard as he strode down the hall.

"Good evening, Your Majesty, Lady Vera," he greeted, then took his place behind them. As was protocol, members of the royal family always had a Dragon Guard escort wherever they went. Usually, one was stationed outside the queen's offices, too, but Vera guessed they were shorthanded with Niklas away. She didn't even think that there might be a chance it would be Stein standing guard when she approached the queen's offices. Thank the gods, as she wasn't prepared to have that confrontation.

However, it seemed the gods weren't quite with her. As soon as they turned the corner, she immediately spotted the tall, imposing figure standing right outside the entrance to the royal apartments. Her stomach leapt into her throat and stayed lodged the entire length of the long, slow walk to the door.

Her pulse thrummed in her veins as they drew nearer. Stein looked so fierce in his Dragon Guard attire and armor. It suited him so much more than the coat and tie he'd sported in Paris. His long braid draped over one shoulder; his steely glare fixed ahead. His rigid body remained unmoving, still and silent as a rock. This was usual for him, of course. But some secret part of her hoped that after Paris, seeing each other again would be *un*usual enough for him that he would acknowledge her existence in some way like a secret glance or a tick in his strong jaw muscles as she walked by. Vera's heart plummeted back to earth.

"Thank you, Rorik," Queen Sybil said, dismissing the captain. "Say hi to Poppy for me, will you? And tell her I'm *not* missing your wedding, even if I have to keep my legs crossed."

The stolid Dragon Guard look flustered. "Of course, Your Majesty. But if you did, we would completely understand." He put his fist over his heart, bowed, and then turned and left.

"Can you believe it's so close to Poppy and Rorik's wedding?" Queen Sybil eased herself onto the plush couch in the middle of the living area. "Now that you're back, you'll attend, right?"

"Of course." The mention of weddings had Vera's throat drying up.

The queen kicked off her shoes and propped her feet up on the antique gold and marble coffee table. "Now, what's this appointment about, Vera? You know you can just pop by anytime for a chat. You're always welcome here."

"I know. But I wanted to talk to you about—"

"Ooh, Alric, there you are!" Despite her burgeoning belly, the queen shot to her feet when the nanny entered with the prince. She waddled over to them and took her son in her arms. "Did you miss me, baby? I missed you." She rained kisses all over his face, which made the child giggle and squeal, then carried him back to the couch with her. "Sorry about that. What were you saying?"

"Er, yes. I wanted to—" She stopped short, feeling her chest compress in on itself as she watched Prince Alric babble happily as his mother doted on him. Her gaze dropped down to the queen's pregnant belly. The words to ask the queen for help with Lisbet escaped her.

Why did I even come here?

The solution to her problem had been bundled into a neat package, tied with a bow, and dropped on her lap. If she married Tobi, she would have *this*. The life she'd always wanted. All she had to do was say *yes*.

"Vera?" The queen cocked her head to the side.

"Yes." The lump in her throat fought its way down as she swallowed it. "I wanted you to be the first to know my news. I'm getting married. To Jarl Armundson. Tobi."

"Married? To Jarl Armundson?" The queen's jaw practically unhinged. "Why?"

"I beg your pardon, Your Majesty? Do you not approve?"

"It's not that, Vera. This ... I mean, at the luncheon you were being so secretive about him when I asked you." She motioned for the nanny to come back and take Alric again. Once they were safely squired away in the nursery, she scooted closer to Vera. "And now you're telling me you're getting married. Forgive me, but this seems so out of left field, especially for you."

"I ... I wasn't sure of my answer when he asked me." Staring into the dragon queen's silvery eyes proved difficult, as if Queen Sybil would be able to ferret the truth out if she met her gaze. So Vera focused on the spot between her dark eyebrows. "I asked for time, and then I made my decision."

"Does this have anything to do with Paris?"

The question hit her like a wallop to the chest. Did she suspect that something happened between her and Stein? Did the Dragon Guard tell her? "W-what do you mean, Your Highness?"

"I mean, getting kidnapped and having a near-death experience can change you. And that was only last week. Maybe you're still in shock? That's why you're making rash decisions?"

"I beg your pardon?" Vera tried her damndest not to sound defensive, but the queen's words hit their target too closely. "Surely it's possible to fall in love with someone in a matter of weeks. Didn't you fall in love with King Aleksei in a few days?"

"That's different."

"Because you're mates and shifters?"

"I—" Queen Sybil's mouth pressed together. "I'm sorry, Vera, if I sound harsh. Of course I'm happy for you. I really am, if you love him."

Vera bit the inside of her cheek to stop herself from correcting the queen. "Thank you."

"And I'll support you in any way I can, of course. Both Aleksei and I will." She winked at Vera. "Surely in a year, I'll be able to bounce back from giving birth, and I'll be there to attend. Maybe even be a bridesmaid?"

A year? If hadn't even occurred to Vera that wedding preparations might take that long. No, that was impossible. Not if the adoption would take over a year.

"Actually, Tobi and I would like to get married as soon as possible." They hadn't discussed dates yet, but surely now that he knew she wanted to start the adoption process right away, he'd agree to a quick wedding. "We'll have a simply ceremony at Heddal Church, then a wedding breakfast." She mentally crossed her fingers that Tobi and his mother would agree.

The queen's eyebrows went all the way up to her hairline. "That's really ..." Her gaze dropped to Vera's belly. "You're not—"

"N-no!" she sputtered, wrapping her arms around her middle. "I'm not. Also, I don't want to overshadow Poppy's wedding. A-and Tobi and I have known each other for so long, we don't want to wait any longer."

Queen Sybil's gaze narrowed, but she shrugged. "I ... all right. Will you be making the announcement soon? May I tell Aleksei?"

"Yes, you may tell His Majesty. Um, but would you mind waiting the day after tomorrow? We need to tell our parents the news first." And also accept her future fiancé's proposal.

"Of course." The queen enveloped her in a tight hug. "I'm happy for you, Vera. I'm so glad you're getting what you want."

That lump in her throat returned. "Th-thank you."

They chatted for a few more minutes until Vera asked to be excused, citing that she had to prepare for her dinner. The queen walked her out of the apartments, and to her relief, Stein was gone from his post, replaced by Gideon.

Sitting in the back of her limo, she slipped her phone out of her purse. Her fingers hovered over the call icon on the screen, until she silently screamed at her thumb to just *press the godsdamn thing*.

Two rings later, Tobi picked up. "Vera?"

"Yes," she blurted out.

"I beg your pardon?"

"My answer to your question"—she swallowed hard—"is yes."

The dead air stretched for half a heartbeat. "I ... I don't know what to say. I mean, that's wonderful, darling. I'm so happy."

"Yes, me too." It sounded like the right thing to say. "But, Tobi, I don't want to wait. Do you think we could get married as soon as possible? You don't mind, do you?"

"Mind?" he chuckled. "Do I mind that you can't wait to be my wife? Of course not. We'll do it as soon as we can book the church."

"Wonderful." The words rang hollow to her ears. "I'll tell my father tonight, and you can tell your mother. Then, why don't you and Countess Armundson come over to dinner tomorrow night so we can celebrate?"

"Sounds like a plan. Darling, you've made me the happiest man in the world."

"I'm glad." There was a pause, as if he was waiting for her to say something else. "So, I'll speak with you soon, Tobi."

"I'll think of you until then, darling."

Vera lowered her hand and sank back into her seat, the energy draining out of her. *You can do this*, she told herself. Most of the hard part was done. All that was left was to tell her father.

And actually get married.

Staring out the window, the streets of the historic district blurred by, the old buildings and walls melding into each other. She tried to imagine Tobi's handsome face and bright blue eyes looking at her with happiness on her wedding day.

But for the life of her, she couldn't picture it. Instead, another image kept popping in front of her. Craggy, harsh lines. Piercing steel gray eyes. The hard line of the mouth that kissed her senseless, not only once but twice now.

Her chest hurt just thinking about him, but what was she supposed to do? She couldn't make Stein want her *and* want children any more than she could command the flowers to grow in winter or the sun to rise at midnight.

I have to move on with my life and be happy. For Lisbet, and for herself.

CHAPTER 8

"Stein, I need to pull you out of today's roster."

Stein had barely stepped out of his apartment when he heard the words. He didn't even bother looking at Rorik when he replied with a firm, *No.*

The captain ran his palm down his face. "Do not be difficult, Stein. Not today."

How am I being difficult? We are shorthanded as it is with Niklas away. He snorted. *I will guard the king today.*

"First of all, you have been on duty non-stop for the last two weeks," Rorik pointed out.

So?

"You know that according to the rules, you need at least one day of rest every six days of duty. It's been two weeks since you returned, and you've not had any day off."

It's just you, me, and Gideon here right now, and between us we must guard the king, queen, Prince Alric, Prince Harald, Prince Sasha, and Princess Iyavana. None of us have had time to rest.

"Which brings me to my second point. Niklas and

Annika have just returned, along with Princess Alyx and Prince Mikhail."

Mother Frigga.

"So, see? We now have more than enough personnel to cover everyone."

I will stay as backup.

Rorik let out a frustrated grunt. "Stein, will you—" He paused and crossed his arms over his chest. "Fine. But you're on duty with the queen today."

Fuck.

Since he returned from Paris, Stein had done nothing but work, doing double duty shifts every day. When he did have a few hours of free time, he went to the Dragon Navy and trained with them until he'd exhausted himself so much, he would collapse back in his bed in a dreamless sleep.

It was the only way he could stop himself and his dragon from seeking out Vera. Of course, there was a chance she'd come back to the palace again, so he made sure to only sign up for duty with the king or Prince Harald. If he'd noticed it, Rorik didn't say a word. But it seems he did notice.

Fine, he grumbled. *Why are the prince and princess back anyway?*

"The wedding," Rorik stated.

Wedding? As far as Stein knew, Rorik and Poppy's wedding was two weeks away. It seemed rather early, but perhaps the siblings had missed their parents.

"You have the next two days off," Rorik said.

Two days? Stein would have to swim all the way to Greenland to prevent his dragon from going crazy. *What am I supposed to do?*

"Whatever it is you do when you're off duty." Rorik

waved his hand dismissively. "You are relieved of your post starting immediately. Oh, and by the way, I've already contacted Admiral Horik and told him you are not to be allowed to train with the navy."

Damn nosy Rorik.

All right.

Perhaps Niklas or Annika would be up for some training, especially since he doubted they'd had any time while they worked on the security plans for Princess Alyx.

Without another word, he strode off in the direction of the east wing of the royal apartments, where he guessed Niklas and Annika would proceed first as they likely missed their brood of five adopted children. Sure enough, when he got there, the entire party—Niklas, Annika, Princess Alyx, Prince Mikhail, and the two guards were just arriving.

Niklas, I must speak with you.

"Stein, nice to see your friendly face," Niklas joked. "To what do I owe this—"

"You!" Princess Alyx marched toward him with ground-eating steps. "This is your fault!" Her face scrunched up as she placed her hands on her hips, her neck craning back to glare at him.

"I beg your pardon?"

Ranulf was by her side in an instant and placed a hand on her shoulder. "Alyx, let us go inside. Your parents must be—"

She brushed his hand off. "No! I need to say my piece first."

Stein looked to Ranulf and then Magnus. *What is she talking about?* Unfortunately, his question was answered with silence and stony stares.

"This wedding." She poked a finger at his chest. "This is *your* fault! She wouldn't be doing this if you'd just had the *balls* to tell her how you really feel, you cold-hearted asshole!"

Now he was confused. "Why would I have anything to do with Rorik and Poppy's wedding?"

"Rorik and Poppy?" The princess cocked her head to the side. "You don't know, do you?"

"Know what?" he asked, impatient.

"We're not back for Poppy and Rorik's wedding," she said. "We're here for Vera's wedding tomorrow."

At first Stein thought he must have heard it wrong. But the sympathetic glances from Magnus and Ranulf confirmed it.

Mine! His dragon shrieked. In fact, it was so loud that all four dragons in the room started.

Stein? Niklas asked, his jaw dropping. *Is she—*

"Shut up!" he roared. *Say another word—any of you and you'll regret it!* "Is this true?" he asked Ranulf.

The Dragon Guard nodded.

"She's desperate to adopt Lisbet," Princess Alyx began. "But the courts won't let her because she's a single woman."

"That's the law," Niklas said, rubbing his jaw. "But surely the queen and king could help her?"

"That's what I said," Alyx retorted, exasperated. "But Jarl Armundson must have gotten to her before she could ask them and offered to marry her so they could adopt Lisbet. I mean, that's the only explanation for this shotgun wedding, right? Adoptions could take months. Years even, so she would want to start right away."

Blood rushed into his ears, the deep roar nearly deafening. He knew exactly which child she wanted to adopt—the tiny waif with the sad blue eyes and the blonde pigtails. After all, he did nothing but watch her each time they were in the same room, and because of his duties, it was often when the queen was visiting the Children's Foundation.

So, she wanted to adopt the girl. Possibilities filled his head. He could have given her what she wanted while keeping his vow. He could do that for her.

But no, Vera would want children of her own too. He'd seen the envious way she looked at the queen's pregnant belly. And she deserved that. A husband who could give her everything she wanted.

Stein, Niklas said. *If she is your—*

He slammed down the barriers of their mental link then spun on his heel. He didn't know which direction he was going, but he didn't care, because if he didn't leave the palace, his dragon would riot.

As soon as he stepped outside, his dragon ripped out of him. Its mighty feet pushed off the ground, and they took off into the sky. He wanted to stop his dragon from reaching its destination, but at the same time, he had to confirm it for himself. And so, he let it fly like an arrow soaring to its target until he landed outside at the Solveigson manor.

Cloaking himself, he swiftly climbed up the trellis on the side all the way to the terrace just outside his mate's bedroom. The glass doors had been left open, the sheer curtains fluttering invitingly. His hearing immediately picked up the sound of voices as they drifted out the doors, and unable to help himself, he crept in. Razor wire wrapped around his throat at the sight that greeted him.

"You look beautiful, dear," Jarl Solveigson said.

No, his mate was stunning, but all his insides knotted themselves seeing her standing in front of the full-length mirror, dressed in the white gown. The one she was to wear when she married another tomorrow.

"Thank you, Father." Her hands smoothed down the white gauzy fabric of her skirt, then turned to face him. "And thank you for everything."

"I told you, I would support you in whatever you want to do. And Tobi is from a good family. We've known the Armundsons for years." His white brows knitted together. "You know I love you, right?"

"Of course." She strode over to him and clasped his hands in his. "I do worry now that you'll be alone in this big house. But I shall come by every day if I'm able, but if not, you'll have to come visit me."

"Bah, do not worry about me." He sat her down on the bed. "I say this because I care about you and love you. But there is no need to rush into marriage. And there is still time."

Hope flared in Stein's chest.

She sighed. "Why does everyone think I'm making a rash decision? I've known Tobi since we were children."

"I know, dear. I just don't want you to be trapped in a marriage because you feel like you have no choice."

"Pappa, this isn't about *her*, you know."

Jarl Armundson's face paled. "Some people say marrying your mother was the biggest mistake of my life. And I do regret not interfering ... with the way she'd treated you growing up." He shook his head. "But without her, I wouldn't have you."

Vera's eyes glittered with tears. "Then you know why I have to do this. If you had a choice, you wouldn't change anything would you, even if it meant saving yourself from the heartbreak of your marriage?"

The old man sighed. "Not for all the treasure in the world."

Slowly, he backed out of the room, the razor wire tightening around his throat with each step.

He often wondered what made Vera change her ways over the last three years from a spoiled, selfish brat to a kind, selfless person. Now he knew. He'd seen the look of love in her dark violet eyes when she gazed on the child. The one that proclaimed that her heart had chosen this person, and it would not settle for less. He envied it, yet understood.

And she didn't deserve anything less than everything she wanted.

So, despite his dragon's protestations, he knew he had to let her go. Because he could never make Vera truly happy.

"You're the biggest idiot in the Northern Isles."

Stein didn't bother to look behind him. It was Niklas, of course. He should have known the tenacious Dragon Guard would hound him once his secret came out.

"Well? What have you got to say for yourself?"

How did you find me?

It was a fair question, seeing as he'd been gone for nearly twenty-four hours. After what had transpired at the Solveigson estate, he's shifted into dragon form and flew off. He circled the Northern Isles several times, by air and by sea, until he grew tired. Then he came here and laid down on the soft grass, watching the sun rise.

"With much difficulty," Niklas answered as he stepped up beside him. "So, this is where you go to brood?"

He looked over the Cliffs of Skruor, staring into the horizon.

"This is where it all began, right? The day of the attack when you broke off?"

Stein grunted. It had been far longer than that.

"What in Hel are you doing, Stein?" Niklas grabbed his bicep and spun him so they stood face-to-face. "You're just going to stand here brooding and let her marry another man?"

He tugged his arm away violently. *Don't touch me.*

"Why, Stein? Why are you denying yourself and your dragon the chance to be happy with a mate? Are you some kind of masochist? Why let your animal suffer because you're too stubborn to take what you want?"

I don't owe you an explanation, he spat.

"And her? You don't think she deserves to know that she's your *mate*?"

He grit his teeth. *You don't understand. I can't.*

"Why?"

"I just can't!" he roared. "I don't deserve her."

Niklas guffawed. "Do you think any of us deserve our mates? Annika's the most amazing woman in the world, and I'm not worthy to kiss the ground she walks on. Yet, somehow, the gods deemed her to be mine. And she chose to be with me even though she could have done so much better." He paused to take a deep breath. "You know you can't deny this. Your souls know it, and if you let her marry someone else, you'll regret it for the rest of your life."

She might not even want me.

"Did she tell you that, or did you convince yourself?"

Stein ground his teeth together. *Leave me alone, Niklas.*

The other dragon let out a sigh. "Fine. But if you change your mind, the ceremony starts in an hour. Heddal Church. The bride usually waits in one of the anterooms at the entrance before they begin." Without another word, Niklas disappeared.

Stein turned back toward the sea. Despite his calm exterior, his dragon raged at him from the inside.

We can't, he told his beast. *We could never make her happy.*

The dragon roared even louder, the shriek bursting his eardrums.

Stop this insanity!

Talons dug into his insides, bleeding him.

"Fine," he shouted. Perhaps the only way to get his dragon to accept that Vera could never be theirs was to make his dragon see it with its very own eyes. And so, he leapt off the cliff, swiftly changing into his animal form inches before he hit the ground.

His dragon's wings flapped desperately in the direction of the city, toward the spires of Heddal Church that called to them like a beacon. Landing on the marble steps, he Cloaked himself and slipped into the anteroom just to the left of the entrance.

"Aren't we starting yet?"

"Soon, Mother."

Stein cursed silently as he saw the handsome man in the tuxedo. *Wrong room.*

So, this was Jarl Armundson. He recognized him from the luncheon at the Children's Foundation, when he sat next to Vera, leaning so close to her that he wanted to rip the bastard's head off from his spine. *And the pinch-faced matron must be his mother.*

The regal woman sat on a chaise to the side, back ramrod straight, hands folded in her lap. She looked up at the clock impatiently. "Is it time yet?"

Armundson frowned. "No, same as the last five times you asked."

She let out an impatient breath. "I'm so glad Vera didn't want a fancy reception with long toasts and speeches and dances."

"And that she wanted to get married right away?" He snorted and leaned back against the windowsill, arms folding over his chest. "So that you can get your hands on her money as soon as the ink dries on the marriage contract?"

Stein's blood froze in his veins.

What. The. Fuck.

"Don't be so crass, Tobias," Countess Armundson chided. "It's very unbecoming."

The jarl straightened his stance and glared at his mother. "So was gambling away our family fortune, but that didn't stop Father, did it?"

The countess's cold facade didn't even crack. "In thirty minutes, it won't matter. She will be your wife, and we will have control of not only her dowry, but someday, when her father dies, the Solveigson lands and businesses will be ours as well."

"Just in time, too, as the wolves are already at the door," he snorted.

"What of the brat?"

"What brat?"

The countess sneered. "The ragamuffin she wants to adopt."

Ice blue eyes narrowed. "Our solicitors are 'working' on that as we speak." He grinned. "A misplaced piece of paper here, a wrong signature there ... the adoption could be tied up in the courts for years. Long enough for the little guttersnipe to age out of the system."

That. Rotten. Bastard!

It took all of Stein's strength not to shift into his dragon and eat him alive. His beast, on the other hand, was already making plans on how to make the asshole hurt before crunching on his bones and devouring his flesh.

"Our problems will all be over soon." Countess Armundson stood up and went to her son to straighten his tie. "You're a genius for thinking up this plan."

"I'm glad I got your brains and not Father's."

Stein couldn't take any more of this. He marched out of the room, slamming the door behind him, not caring that they heard him. Looking ahead, he saw the door across the hall.

His chest squeezed tight, knowing who was inside that other room. He didn't hesitate, not now, because he'd be damned if he let that scumbag take advantage of Vera. Grabbing the door handle, he flung it open and marched inside.

"Is it—Stein?" A white-gloved hand went to her throat.

Gods, but she was even lovelier today, dressed in that white gown. Her dark shiny hair was piled atop her head, her lush lips parted in a gasp, and those dark violet eyes wide with surprise as they stared at each other.

"W-what are you doing here?" she asked, her voice trembling.

"You cannot marry him."

Her complexion lost all its color. "I-I can't?"

"No."

"Why not?"

"Because he is using you." He reached her in two strides. "I was in the other room, and I overheard him and his insufferable mother. He doesn't love you; he's broke and needs your money. That, and he has no intention of adopting Lisbet. He's instructed his solicitors to intentionally mishandle the adoption."

"W-hat?"

"I said he's—"

"I heard what you said." She swallowed hard. "It can't be true. It's not. He promised me. Why are you doing this?" Color heightened her cheeks. "Y-you were the one who walked away from me, and now you think you can just come here on my wedding day and try to take this away from me too?"

"Vera, I'm telling the truth." He scrubbed his hand down his face. "You can't marry him. You'll be miserable."

"And how would you know what being miserable is like?" she accused.

If only she knew. "Don't marry him." *Please.* "He'll make sure you never adopt Lisbet."

Her lips pressed together. "Even if that were true, I can always hire my own solicitors. And I don't care about the money."

Of course she didn't. Because that was who she was now. To her, the welfare of the child came first. The daughter of her heart.

"Why are you really here, Stein?"

The question took him off guard. "To save you from making a grave mistake."

Her nostrils flared. "As you can see, I'm perfectly fine and in no need of saving."

She was right. Vera was an adult. She could make her own decisions.

Mine, his dragon cried. *Mine.*

Pain buried in his chest like a great axe cleaving him in two.

"Stein, why can't you just tell me the truth?"

His head shot up to meet her gaze. Those hypnotizing dark violet eyes looked at him pleadingly, and his pulse shot up.

"I shouldn't want you still." A soft sob escaped her throat as she drew closer to him. "But for the life of me, I can't stop thinking about you. Why?" A hand reached out, but she dropped her arm to her side when he flinched away. "What is it about you that you're all I think about? That I dream of your kisses. And more."

His emotions raged like a hurricane inside him. "We will not suit."

"I know. I want Lisbet and other children, and you don't. That's fair. But why? What have you got against having children?"

The razor wire around his throat came back, though in truth, it had never left. Perhaps if she understood, she would let this go. Cold sweat broke out on his forehead at what he was about to do, but he had no other choice but to tell her the truth.

"My father was a terrible person, born of terrible people," he began. "He was scum. Lower than scum, coming from a family of good for nothings. Criminals, every last one of them." He closed his eyes. "He's sitting in a prison on Jokulsa island. Lifetime sentence. No parole."

Vera gasped. She must have known that the maximum-security facility on the remote island on the western tip of the country was reserved for the truly worst of the worst criminals.

"He murdered my mother while she was trying to defend me from another one of his beatings," he said before she got the chance to ask. "He killed her right in front of me."

She let out a cry, but he held up a hand to stop her. "And so I vowed to her, as I held her dead body in my arms, that I would never, ever let another child go through what I did. The cycle ends with me. House of Kvalheim ends with me."

"Stein—"

"You don't want me, Vera. Not my tainted blood or name. That name would follow my children wherever they went. Everyone would ridicule them, call them scum. Deserters. Criminals." Unable to bear to look at her face—which was likely filled with horror and disdain—he turned away from her. "Marry him or not, promise me that if there is anything you can do to secure the child, do it." After all, he knew what it was like to be unwanted. Passed from one unloving family to another.

"So that's it?" She marched over to face him. To his surprise, she wasn't horrified or disgusted. No, her eyes blazed with pure fury. "You think just because your father was a bad person, you can't be different? You're not him, Stein." She paused, her lips pressing together tightly. "You're not giving yourself credit for all the good you've done, all the lives you've saved. All the work you've put in over the years to ensure you don't turn out bad, despite the so-called tainted blood and legacy you claim to have."

"Why do you care?"

"Why do I care?" Tears filled her eyes. "Gods know ... because if you can't believe you can change despite your upbringing, then that means *I* can't either. It means I can't get past my own programming and be a better person. A worthy mother who will protect and care for her child instead of destroying her." She sniffed and turned away from him. "You know what? Go ahead and walk out that door. I'll be just fine."

"Vera—"

"I said go!"

His dragon didn't want to leave her, but he had no choice. "As you wish." Cloaking himself, he trudged out the door.

Outside, it was a beautiful, sunny morning. The perfect day for a wedding. He could already imagine the bells of Heddal ringing in a joyful tune once the bride and groom walked out the door.

I have to get out of here.

And so, he shifted and flew off, getting lost in the bright blue sky, trying to block out his mate's voice repeating in his head.

You don't give yourself credit.

All the good you've done.

Because if you can't change, that means I can't either.

If only there was some kind of medical procedure or magic spell that could make him forget her words. But they burrowed into his brain, as well as the image of her standing in her wedding dress, eyes filled with tears.

Was change really possible?

Of course it was. She proved that. He'd witnessed her transformation.

But how about him? The blood of those before him ran deep. Could he possibly put the past behind him—his fears, his doubts?

Niklas's words from earlier that morning came back to him. None of them were worthy of their magnificent mates.

Could he be worthy enough for her?

And the answer came to him in a whisper from deep within.

CHAPTER 9

S tein had disappeared just in time, right before her father entered the anteroom.

"Vera, are you all right? You look pale as a ghost." He rushed to her side and placed a hand on her brow.

"I-I'm fine, Pappa," she stammered. Her entire body felt numb, but somehow, she managed to take her father's offered arm and followed him outside.

"You make a beautiful bride, my dear," he said as he handed her the bouquet sitting on top of the table by the exit.

Her father's warm smile gave her a modicum of comfort. "Th-thank you, Pappa," she managed to say despite the tightness in her throat.

"You've grown up into an exceptional young woman." His eyes shimmered with tears. "And I'm so very proud of you."

"That means a lot." She swallowed the bitterness gathering in her throat. This would have to be enough. Her father's love and adoration. Lisbet by her side. And maybe she'd learn to love Tobi someday.

Stein's words, however, echoed in her brain. Was he really telling the truth? Had Tobi and his family lost their fortune? Was he really going to stop her from adopting Lisbet?

Before she could ponder further, the large wooden doors to the church swung open. The rusty hinges sounded much louder to her ears, as if they signaled something ominous. Thankfully, the organ music that played the bridal march drowned out the sound, as well as her thoughts.

Her knees were like jelly, so she leaned onto her father for support. Up ahead, Tobi waited for her at the end of aisle, looking handsome and polished in his tux. This was her wedding day. She should be happy. But all she could think about was Stein.

Was Tobi really using her for her money?

Did it matter? She was using him so she could adopt Lisbet, even if it was with his consent. She didn't care about the money, as long as she had enough to live on. And none of her father's business interests or lands would fall to her until he passed on, which she hoped would be a very long time from now.

But what if he found a way to sabotage the adoption, even if she hired her own solicitors?

"Dearly beloved, we are gathered here today before the All-Father Odin and all the gods ..."

Vera nearly had whiplash as her head snapped to Tobi, who stood beside her. Did the ceremony really start? She had no recollection of reaching the end of the aisle nor of her father handing her over to her groom. Now, they were standing in front of the altar as Archpriestess Heikkinen recited the words that would forever bind her to Tobi.

"The sacred vows of marriage are not to be taken lightly," the archpriestess continued. "Therefore—"

A loud crash followed by a strong gust of wind blew through the church. Vera swung her head back down the aisle as the air shimmered with an unknown energy. She didn't need to wait for the large figure to fully materialize to know who it was. Her stomach did flips at the sight of Stein marching down the aisle with purposeful steps.

"What is the meaning of this?" King Aleksei, who was sitting at the very front pew on the bride's side, shot to his feet. "Stein, I order you to leave."

The hulking Dragon Guard halted and faced his king, placing a hand over his chest. "Respectfully, Your Majesty, this is the one command I cannot follow."

King Aleksei made a move to spring toward Stein, but stopped short. Vera's gaze dropped down to the queen's hand on his arm. To Vera's shock, the king actually sat back down.

"What's going on?" Tobi exclaimed. "You! Who the Hel do you think you are?" Stomping down the dais, he blocked Stein's path. To his credit, he didn't appear intimidated despite the fact that the Dragon Guard was over half a foot taller and probably thirty pounds heavier.

Stein, however, didn't even spare him a glance. In fact, his granite gaze fixed right on Vera. "You cannot marry him."

A collective gasp rose from the guests.

Vera thought she was experiencing some kind of déjà vu as he repeated the same words from earlier. Breathless, she simply replied. "Why?"

"Because you are mine."

Shock and awareness washed over her like a wave. The words didn't make sense, but somehow ... they *did*.

"You are my mate, Vera. The one the gods destined to be mine. The other half of my soul."

"M-mate?" Helpless, she looked over to the very frontmost pews where her father and friends sat. They, however, were unable to offer any assistance as their expressions ranged from surprise to shock to dumbfounded. Indeed, she'd never seen King Aleksei look quite so ... *un*regal with his mouth wide open.

"Yes," Stein replied.

Mate. He was her *mate*. "You've known for the last three years, and you didn't say anything?"

"No."

"Oh."

"I've known for six years, three months, two weeks, five days. Since the first moment I saw you during the King and Queen's Ball during the Landing Day celebrations."

That had been the first time she attended an event at Helgeskar Palace after her coming out in Paris. Had he really known since then?

"Vera!" Tobi rushed back to her side. "Are you really going to believe this ... this overgrown oaf? You made a promise to me. We must get on with the wedding." He turned to the king. "Your Majesty, tell your manservant to leave at once!"

"Are you giving me an order, Jarl Armundson?" The king did not move an inch, but the coldness and power in his tone changed the tenor inside the church.

Tobi swallowed audibly. "N-no, Your Majesty. But she is my bride. We've already signed all the paperwork. You must agree, this is not done."

"True," King Aleksei conceded. "But I will allow it. For

even I cannot go against the will of the gods."

Tobi's face turned scarlet. "This is outrageous," he sputtered. "Vera, you can't possibly believe what this madman is saying."

She turned her gaze from Stein to Tobi. "Is it true that you've lost your fortune?"

If it was possible, he turned even redder. "I didn't. My father did," he admitted. "But I never deceived you or pretended I wasn't having financial problems."

"You lied by omitting the truth," she retorted. "And were you going to sabotage the adoption?"

The jarl's mouth opened and shut like a carp gasping for air in land. "I-I-I—Vera, please. We can fix this." His desperation reeked in the air like a cloying perfume. "I'll do anything you want. You can hire your own people for the adoption, I promise I won't interfere."

Vera thought the confirmation would break her heart, but sadly, she knew Stein was telling the truth the moment he told her. "I'm sorry—" She shook her head. "No, actually, you know what?" She threw her bouquet on the floor. "I'm not sorry. I'm not apologizing to a selfish pig like you!"

"Woohoo!"

Vera suppressed a laugh as Alyx raised a fist in the air.

"Er, sorry," the princess said sheepishly. "Keep going, Vera. You stopped at the 'selfish pig like you.'"

"I will not stand here and be insulted." Tobi stamped his foot with each word. "Vera, I'm giving you one last chance to change your mind. Otherwise, I'm walking out that door and you'll never see me again."

Vera folded her arms over her chest. "Is that a threat or a promise?"

Before Tobi could say anything, Stein stormed up the dais and placed himself between her and her now ex-groom. Because of his bulk, Vera couldn't see his or Tobi's face nor hear what Stein whispered to the other man, but whatever it was, it was enough to make Tobi gasp and then turn tail.

"Mother, we're leaving!" he announced as he scrambled down to his side of the church.

"Don't let the door hit you on the way out!" Alyx snickered.

"Oh dear." Vera didn't know if she wanted to laugh or die from embarrassment as every single pair of eyes in the church gawked at her. "W-what do we do now?"

Stein turned back to her, further blocking her view. "Let me take care of this." He paused, his eyebrows knitting together as if he were thinking. Someone from the front pew immediately stood up.

"Hey, folks!" Niklas waved his hands and ran up to the front of the aisle. "First of all, thanks for joining us this morning. Unfortunately, today's ceremony has been canceled—for obvious reasons. Starting with the groom's side, we ask that you please file out in an orderly manner ..."

Vera giggled at the absurdity of it all. When she lifted her head to meet Stein's steely gray eyes, her breath caught in her throat.

Her mate.

They were mates.

Her stomach fluttered in excitement. More than that, there was a sense of rightness within her.

But that didn't mean she wasn't seriously incensed. So, when Stein began to lean down, she stopped him with a raised hand.

"Why didn't you say anything?" She placed her hands on her hips. "Because of who I was? How I acted back then?"

He at least had the courtesy of looking ashamed. "I will not lie to you, Vera. Ever. And I will spend the rest of my days asking for your forgiveness, but yes. You barely looked at me that first time we crossed paths. And when I realized you had your heart set on Aleksei and being queen, I thought it best to not say anything."

Gods, she was a nightmare back then. How could she blame him for steering clear of her? "I was a terrible, selfish person. I don't have any excuses for my past behavior, and I won't make any." Her mother, after all, had died long before she first met Aleksei. She could have chosen to be a good person, yet even in death, she wanted to prove Erika Solveigson wrong. That she was worthy of being loved and cherished. "But I've changed now."

"I know. I believe it," he whispered, his tone so achingly tender. "And if you can change, so can I. And I can change my mind too."

She searched his face for the meaning of his words. "Does that mean ... you'll want children?"

"As many as you can give me," he replied without missing a beat. "And of course, Lisbet will be our first. Our daughter of the heart."

Happiness burst from within her, and she practically leapt up at him. He recovered quickly and caught her, wrapping his arms around her waist, then lifted her up to bring their mouths together. The fluttering in her stomach intensified as his lips moved desperately over hers.

"Hey, guys?" Alyx's voice made them pull apart. "Maybe

you should go somewhere private before things get too hot and heavy?"

Stein muttered something unintelligible under his breath.

Vera could hardly suppress her smile. "If you wouldn't mind ...?" With a sharp nod, he placed her back on her feet. "Thank you." Glancing back out across the room, she saw it was nearly empty except for the first two rows on the bride's side. The king, queen, the rest of the royal family, her father, and the Dragon Guards and their mates remained in their seats.

She cleared her throat. "Um, I guess we should all go home? Since there won't be a wedding today." Or a wedding breakfast, since that was supposed to take place at the Armundson estate.

"That doesn't have to be the case."

"What?" Her head swung back to Stein. "What do you mean, that doesn't—" She inhaled on a gasp. "Stein?"

"Marry me, Vera."

She waited for the punchline, but it never came. This was Stein, after all. "Here? *Now*?"

"Yes." His serious tone matched his expression. "We are in a church. You are in a dress. And you are my mate. Let's get married. Now."

Flabbergasted, she turned to Archpriestess Heikkinen. "Is that even possible?"

The wizened old woman shook her head. "I am sorry, Lady Vera. I mean, I could perform the ceremony, but it won't be legally binding because the paperwork is in Jarl Armundson's name. You could apply for a new license and have it approved in a week."

Disappointment filled her. "Well," she began, "I guess—"

"*Yeow!*"

All eyes turned back to the front pew as Gideon shot to his feet. "Niklas, what the Hel? Why did you pinch me?"

"Bro ..." Niklas nodded at Vera and Stein, then cocked his head toward the king.

"What?" Gideon frowned, then his expression shifted. "Oh! According to the laws of the Northern Isles, the sovereign can marry any citizen of the country anywhere within the borders. Such union shall be recognized as true and legal and—wait, is that why you asked me to look up marriage laws last night? How did you know?"

Niklas didn't say anything, except he put his hands behind his head, leaned back, and smiled smugly.

Stein let out a loud grunt. "Your Majesty, would you do us the honor?"

This time, the expression on King Aleksei's face was that of joy. "I would be glad to."

As she watched His Majesty approach them, all Vera could think of was, *Is this really happening?*

"One moment, Your Majesty." Stein turned to her. "You do want to marry me, do you not?"

"Yes." The lack of hesitation in her answer surprised her. "I do want to marry you." She glanced back at her father, who beamed at her. And when she looked back up at her new groom and very shortly-to-be-husband, her heart nearly burst out of her ribcage as she saw the genuine smile on his face.

"Splendid," King Aleksei exclaimed as he took the place that Archpriestess Heikkinen graciously vacated. "I have never performed this before, so you will all have to bear with me. But I'll do my best." He cleared his throat, and everyone settled in their seats. "Today we stand before the gods in Valhalla to join these two people—our friends—in matrimony. Their lives, hearts, and souls will be forever joined so that from now on, they will be together, embracing their dreams while facing their disappointments, lifting each other up while accepting the other's shortcomings, and celebrating their triumphs while tackling whatever adversity that may come their way. Because it will all be worth it when they do it together."

"Wow," Alyx stage-whispered. "I didn't know His Majesty was a poet."

"Shhh!" Niklas admonished. "Pipe down, Princess Talks-a-lot."

The corner of the king's mouth kicked up. "So, do you, Stein, take Lady Vera to be your wife, to have and to hold, for richer or poorer, in sickness and in healthy, till death do you part?"

"I do," he answered.

When the king repeated the vow to her, Vera stared up at her mate's face and flashed him her best smile. "I do."

"By the power invested in me as sovereign of the Northern Isles, I now pronounce you, husband and wife." King Aleksei grinned at them. "If you please, Stein."

Vera found herself enveloped in Stein's strong arms once more as she stood on tiptoe to receive his kiss—their first as man and wife. Applause and whoops broke out from their audience.

Oh dear, would she always react this way when they kissed? The butterflies in her stomach returned, but now, she tingled everywhere, too, as a warmth crept over every inch of her body. As he leaned down further, she wrapped her arms around his neck, as if she could possibly press their lips together even further. When His Majesty gave a discreet cough, they broke apart.

"If the newlyweds agree," Queen Sybil announced as she rose from her seat. "We want to invite everyone here for lunch at the palace later. We can have everything ready by noon."

Stein looked at her, and she nodded at the queen. "You are too kind. Thank you, Your Majesty."

"Since we have a few hours, I would like to take my wife on one important stop," Stein said.

"Damn, Stein! Can't wait to get her alone, eh?" Niklas joked, which earned him an elbow jab from Annika.

Vera's body temperature was just returning to normal but now it shot back up again. Frankly, with the preparations for the ceremony, she hadn't even thought that tonight was her wedding night. In fact, she and Tobi had agreed that they were going to wait before consummating their marriage, a decision that had filled her with relief, rather than disappointment.

Stein glared at the blond Dragon Guard. "Get your mind out of the gutter." Leaning down, he whispered in her ear. "Would you mind flying somewhere with me before we join everyone at the palace, my wife?"

Vera didn't know which made her more giddy—the fact that she would finally go flying with Stein or that he called her his wife. "Not at all."

Hand in hand, they made their way down the aisle as their family and friends cheered them on. Once outside, she followed him toward the square in front of the church.

"I regret not being the first to fly you back in France," he confessed. "But from now on, I'll be the only one to take you to the skies."

She smiled shyly at him. "You'll be the only one I want." Her mouth went dry at the double meaning. "To fly me, I mean."

Moving behind her, he slipped his arms around her waist. "Hold on tight."

Vera closed her eyes as her feet lifted off the ground. Human arms turned into long, scaly ones. Her stomach was left on the ground as they launched upwards.

When she flew with Magnus, she'd been terrified. But somehow, now that she was in Stein's dragon's arms, she felt safer than she did on land. She turned her head to the side. She rubbed her cheek on the cool, leathery scales and was answered with a deep rumble that sounded pleased.

They didn't fly very long, and when they landed on the perfectly manicured lawn outside a red brick building, she instantly recognized where they were. She looked up at him in wonder. "Stein ..."

"We are Cloaked so no one can see us. But I asked Her Majesty if she could call ahead," he said. "She is waiting for you." He gestured to the steps leading up to the main building at the Children's Trust, where Lisbet stood, along with Lara Jacobsen.

"But why are we here?"

"The child doesn't know your plans yet, I assume?"

She shook her head. "No. I was going to ask her once I was sure I could do it."

"Then you should ask her now."

Oh, this man ... how did he know? "I ... I'm nervous. What if she says no?" And if Lisbet did say no, would that mean their wedding would have been for nothing? Would he regret marrying her so impulsively? "Stein ... are you sure you want to do this with me? You don't even know her."

"But I've watched you with her all these years."

"Y-you have?" That's what he had said earlier. He'd been watching her all this time, just waiting at the edges of her life.

"Of course. How can I not watch your every move? When each room you walk into fills with light and every dark corner disappears? And every moment I get to see you makes each day better." He tightened his embrace. "Whatever her answer, I will be here." Releasing her, they rematerialized and walked over.

"Lady Vera!" Lisbet's face broke into a smile, and she ran toward her open arms.

"Oomph!" Vera caught her and lifted her up. "Hello, *lilla du*. How are you?"

When she put Lisbet back down, the girl gasped. "You look so pretty in your dress. Did you wear that just to visit me?"

She chuckled. "You could say that. But I wanted you to be the first to know, I got married today." Glancing back at Stein, she took his hand and pulled him forward. "This is my husband." Her stomach warmed at the words. "Stein, this is Lisbet."

Lisbet's mouth formed into an O. "You're the queen's Dragon Guard."

"Indeed, I am," he replied. "Nice to meet you, Lisbet."

"Lisbet." Vera wiped the sweat building on her palms on the silk of her gown as she bent down to the child's level. "I have a question to ask you."

Blue eyes blinked at her. "What is it?"

"H-how would you feel about being adopted? By me—I mean, us." A warm hand landed on her shoulder. "Would you like that?"

Lisbet's lower lip trembled. "M-my lady ..." A cry escaped her lips, and she once again launched herself into Vera's arms.

Tears pooled in her eyes as she wrapped the child in a fierce hug. "Is that a yes?"

She nodded, rubbing her face on Vera's shoulder.

"I'm so happy," whispered Vera. Happy didn't even begin to describe it. After all, how could one find the right words to describe the moment when one's dreams—and more—came true? Glancing up at Stein, she knew who to thank for this.

"What wonderful news." Mrs. Jacobsen clapped her hands together. "Rest assured, my lady, I will assist you in any way I can."

Vera released Lisbet and stood up. "I appreciate it." She sighed. "I don't suppose we could take Lisbet to our wedding reception?"

"I'm afraid not." Mrs. Jacobsen *tsked* sadly. "You must secure the necessary permissions as she is a minor child and ward of the Queen's Trust."

"I understand," she said, though that didn't make her feel less disappointed.

"We have about two hours before we must leave for the palace," Stein said. "How about we stay here and spend time with her? Would you like that, Lisbet?"

Vera didn't know how her heart didn't just burst out of her chest at that moment. She fought further tears as Lisbet's wary expression shifted into pure happiness.

"T-that would be nice, Mr. Stein."

CHAPTER 10

After having a quick breakfast with Lisbet, they went for a walk in the woods just behind the Children's Trust. Stein stayed a few feet behind the two females as they rambled, not only to allow them privacy, but to give the child space. He could still sense Lisbet's hesitation and wariness toward him, but that was understandable. He was a virtual stranger, after all. But Stein vowed to do what he could to make the child comfortable with him, at the very least. His dragon nodded in agreement, and because his mate already considered Lisbet hers, so did his animal. It would protect and cherish her, just as it would his mate and any of their offspring.

Finally, the hour to leave came. They said their goodbyes to Lisbet, and Vera promised to visit her every day. Instead of flying back, however, the queen had sent her limo to bring them back to the palace.

"Are you disappointed we are not flying?" he asked as he helped her into the limo.

"I do want to fly again," she said. "But I'm not sure my

gown or my hair could survive another trip." She chuckled as she took what was left of the pins in her hair out and shook her locks into waves past her shoulders.

Stein could only watch her in awe. "Have I told you how beautiful you are?" Stein whispered, leaning over toward her.

"Stein ..." Turning her head, she pressed her lips to his.

Unable to help himself, he pulled her onto his lap. Big mistake as his cock jumped at the contact and pressed painfully against his pants. *Calm yourself.* But he was glad for the privacy of the limo, not to mention the time it would afford them, so they could speak privately.

"Vera," he began as he pulled away from her luscious mouth. "Will you come home with me tonight?" He prayed to the gods she understood what he was asking. Being inexperienced himself, he didn't know how to ask a woman—his mate, he reminded himself—to make love with him. "Everything happened quickly, so I understand if you'd like to wait to get to know each other—"

"Yes," she murmured against his mouth. She traced a path of kisses to his ear. "Yes, I would like to go home with you tonight."

It took all his strength not to burst out of the limo and fly her back to his apartment in the North Tower that very moment. His dragon, too, urged him to claim their mate and bond with her, but he tamped it down. Vera should have had a big, fancy wedding with all the pomp and circumstance befitting her stature, and their quickie ceremony was woefully lacking. He wasn't going to deprive her of the chance to celebrate with those nearest and dearest to her.

Soon, the car stopped in front of the palace, and the queen's secretary greeted them and led them to the rear of the palace toward the gardens and all the way to the large glasshouse in the middle.

"What in the world?" Vera gasped as they entered. "It's ... beautiful. Look at the decor!" She pointed to the swathes of white gauzy cloth hanging across the ceiling and walls and the bouquets of white flowers leading down the path to the main part of the conservatory. A long table had been set up with more white decor, ribbons, and shiny silverware.

Stein didn't know the first thing about wedding decorations, but he was happy if his mate was happy.

Applause greeted their arrival as everyone crowded around them. Ignoring the king and his compatriots, he first made a beeline for Jarl Solveigson.

"My lord," he began. "I owe you an apology."

Jarl Solveigson glanced at his daughter before offering his hand. "You owe me nothing, good sir. It is I who owe you for saving my daughter from that dastardly coward."

Stunned, he merely took his new father-in-law's hand and shook it.

"I sent the kitchens and housekeeping into a tizzy trying to get this all set up." Queen Sybil waved to the table. "Let's not let it go to waste."

They all sat down at the table with Stein and Vera in the two middle seats, the king and queen across from them, and the rest of the party scattered around. Despite the formal place settings, the atmosphere was casual and light, filled with laughter and chatter. Stein didn't notice too much, however, because he couldn't keep his eyes off Vera. His *mate*.

Mine, his dragon preened.

And Stein couldn't argue anymore.

You're welcome, Niklas said with a grin as he raised his glass to him.

How in Odin's name did you know? King Aleksei asked.

I had my suspicions from the beginning. He waggled his eyebrows at Stein. *I'm glad I was right.*

Has the bond formed yet? Rorik asked.

The bond?

The mating bond, the captain replied.

He stared at his compatriots. *I ... don't think so.* He'd forgotten about that important component of fated mates—the bond that would form to connect them on a higher level. From what he learned from King Aleksei and the other guards, with the bond, he would not only know if she was nearby, but also feel her emotions.

You would know if it did, Magnus replied. *You would feel her in your very soul.*

All of them nodded or hummed their agreement.

Don't worry, my friend, Gideon assured him. *I'm sure it will only be a matter of time.*

Have you told her you love her yet? Ranulf inquired.

He swallowed. Love? Was he even capable of love? After all these years, after what happened with his mother and father and the events after that, he was sure the ability for that particular emotion had been stripped from his very being. Was that necessary for the bond to form?

We look forward to the day you bond with your mate, King Aleksei said, diplomatic as ever.

What are you men gossiping about? Queen Sybil interjected.

Annika looked pointedly at her mate. *Are you still*

gloating about how you figured out Stein and Lady Vera were mates before he even admitted it?

Tiring of this conversation, Stein shut down the mental link and instead spoke to his mate, leaning close to her ear. "Are you enjoying yourself?"

"Oh yes." Her cheeks turned pink as he nuzzled her softly. "Stein ..."

"Should I stop?"

"No."

"Kiss! Kiss!" Princess Alyx shouted as she clinked her fork against her wine glass. Stein was only happy to oblige as he claimed his mate's mouth once more.

The reception continued on for the rest of the afternoon. Food, wine, and champagne flowed freely, as did the merriment. Niklas appointed himself as best man, much to Stein's consternation, and made a rousing, if embarrassing impromptu speech.

"Not the kitten story," he muttered under his breath as Niklas recounted the tale of how they came upon the poor creature in the river.

"You dove in after the kitten?" Vera asked.

He shrugged. "It needed help. The pathetic little thing would have drowned," he grumbled.

His mate reached up and grabbed the sides of his head and pulled him down for a kiss. It was then he decided that if that's what the story would earn him each time Niklas would tell it, then he didn't mind it too much.

Later on, the children—Niklas and Annika's five adopted kids, Poppy's son Wesley, and of course Prince Alric—joined in the celebration. That made the reception even rowdier as the children ran around the glasshouse, high on the sugar from the three-tiered wedding cake that the palace kitchen had miraculously whipped up on short notice.

"All right, all right!" Niklas called out. "I think it's time to go home, rug rats!"

Moans and cries arose from the protesting children, but their parents won out, and soon, they were ushering their children back to the palace. A few of the guests lingered about, but it was obvious the party was over.

"Did you enjoy yourself?" he asked Vera.

"Oh yes. And you?"

"Definitely." Frankly, they could have had their reception in the middle of a busy street and he would have enjoyed himself because at the end, she would be his. "But I think it's time to retire."

The most beautiful blush crept up into her cheeks. "Will you fly me home?"

"Of course."

After he quickly thanked the king and queen through their mental link, they snuck out of the glasshouse. As he prepared to shift, a thought popped into his head. "My apartment in the North Tower is not fancy or luxurious, but it is clean and comfortable. We could also go to a hotel—"

"No." She clutched his hands tight. "I want to be in your home. In your bed," she added shyly.

Sweet Freya, he could have expired on the spot. And so, with a deep growl, he swept her up into his arms.

Stein had never flown faster in his life, and soon, they entered the North Tower and made their way to his apartment on the first level.

Before Ranulf and Magnus, Stein had actually been the newest addition to the Dragon Guard, so his quarters were the smallest and located on the bottom floor. It was still large compared to his previous living quarters in the Dragon Navy, but it was nothing more than a place to sleep and rest to him. He had kept whatever furniture had been there when he moved in, though he was glad that housekeeping had replaced his mattress a few months ago and provided him with luxurious sheets and pillows every few days.

We should probably talk about living arrangements. Especially since they would soon have a child living with them. But they could figure that out later. In fact, she didn't even notice her surroundings as her eyes were cast down at her feet. When he reached out to touch her cheek, she didn't flinch, but he did notice her tremble.

He tipped her face up. "What's wrong?" Apprehension shone on her face. Did she change her mind? Regret marrying him? "Tell me, please."

"It's nothing." She turned away and wrapped her arms around her middle. "I just ... I'm afraid I won't be able to please you."

Not please him? Was she mad? He almost laughed, from the tension in her spine, he knew that would be the wrong reaction. His instincts told him that there was still something bothering her. If his own childhood experiences taught him anything, long-lasting insecurities came from the person who should have done everything they could to uplift you. "Vera, who made you feel like you were less than you are worth?"

Her shoulders stiffened, but she remained silent. So, he wrapped his arms around her and pulled her against his chest.

"When you said you were brought up to be a selfish person, you meant by your mother, right?"

"How did you—"

"I came to see you the day before your wedding." He winced. "And I overheard you and your father talking about your mother. Forgive me for intruding on your privacy."

Her shoulders tensed further. "It's fine."

"No, it's not." Carefully, he enveloped her in his arms and rested his chin on top of her head. "Tell me."

She relaxed against him. "She-she was not a very nice person. Married my father for his status and money, even though she was fifteen years younger than him. But she was beautiful and vain, and Pappa gave her everything she wanted. Then I was born ... I think she almost resented me. All she did was criticize me."

His jaw tightened. "Go on."

"If I ate too much, she called me fat. If I wasn't dressed or made up properly, she said I was ugly. I tried as hard as I could to please her. To be the best in her eyes. I got the highest grades, got into all the right clubs at school, made friends with all the right people while I looked down my nose at everyone who I thought was beneath me." She blew out a breath. "Still, nothing I did could meet her high standards."

"Sounds like a charming woman," he said snidely.

"Then when I was fifteen, she was diagnosed with a rare blood disease, and she died a year later." She let out what sounded like a sardonic chuckle. "Even facing death, she didn't change, nor was she remorseful. In fact, her vileness had only multiplied. She berated me for every little thing while passing on her 'words of wisdom.' She would often say things like, 'Vera, being nice will get you nowhere' or 'Vera, you either have the best of everything or nothing.' And so ... even after she died, I could hear her voice in my head. Telling me what I had to do. It's silly, right?"

No, it wasn't. And he understood. Except the voice he heard in his head belonged to someone who was still alive. What was that Northern Isles saying? Bad weeds are the hardest to kill.

"And then I met King Aleksei and ..."

The green-eyed monster rose within him, but he pushed it down. She needed to say it as much as he needed to hear it. "It's all right. Go on."

"And I thought, well, if I caught him, that would mean I won, right? That he was the best catch and that voice inside me would finally leave me alone." She drew in a sharp breath. "But then one day, it all changed. The day of the attack, three years ago."

This time, it was he who tensed up.

"I was outside in the garden, looking for a lost little girl who broke away from her principal and her schoolmates. I saw her hiding in the bushes, and I knew I had to bring her to safety."

"Lisbet," he concluded. "Lisbet was the reason you decided to change. She helped banish that voice in your head."

Slowly, she turned to face him, still nestled in his arms. Reaching up, she cupped his face. "Yes. But that's not all. For me, that was the first day I truly met you."

Too stunned to say anything, he could only stare down

into the depths of her dark violet eyes, his dragon rumbling in pleasure.

"Is that ...?"

"Yes." He took one of her hands and placed it over his chest. "My dragon is very happy you're here with us." Lifting her hand back up, he kissed her palm. "And you have nothing to be afraid of. You please me just fine."

"Stein, I-I'm a virgin," she blurted out. "I know it's hard to believe. Tobi and I didn't—"

"Shhh. I do not want his name spoken here. In fact, I would prefer we never speak of him at all." But, oh, the irony of it all. "I don't care if you're a virgin. It wouldn't even matter to me if you were not."

"It wouldn't?"

"Your worth is not tied to your innocence or lack of it."

"You're a shifter," she stated. "I've heard ... stories. About shifter appetites and prowess."

"Vera, ask me when I first slept with someone."

Her lips thinned. "I don't want—"

"Just ask me."

Her nostrils flared. "Fine. When did you first sleep with someone?"

"Tonight, hopefully."

"Ton—what?" She blinked. And then blinked again. "Stein ... you've never ..."

"No."

"Ever?"

"Ever."

"B-but ... how? I mean ..."

"I told you about my vow," he reminded her. "And I take my vow seriously."

"But there are ways to prevent pregnancy."

"I know ... but it didn't feel right. With anyone."

Several heartbeats passed before she spoke. "And now?"

"This"—he embraced her tighter—"*You* are the only thing that feels right."

"Please, Stein," she whispered. "Take me to bed."

How could he possibly say no to that? So, he swept her up into his arms and walked them to his bedroom. His heart raced as he placed her back on her feet by the bed.

She turned to give him her back and pulled her waves of mahogany hair over her shoulder. "Do you mind?"

With how bad his fingers shook, it was a miracle he managed to undo all the tiny pearl buttons on the back of her dress. She shimmied her shoulders and let the sleeves fall down her arms before shrugging off the rest until the fabric pooled at her feet. Unhooking her bra, she let it join the dress on the floor.

He sucked in a breath as his gaze traveled down the length of her naked back, down to the garters, lacy panties, and sheer stockings that showed off her shapely legs.

Facing him, she looked up shyly at him, her arms covering her breasts. "Your turn."

The corner of his mouth kicked up. "Do you mind?" He gestured to his clothes.

She lowered her arms, exposing her lovely breasts to his gaze. Perfectly round, a handful each, tipped with pale pink nipples, he could hardly keep his eyes off them.

Reaching over, her hands made quick work of his shirt buttons, then tugged the material down his arms. He tossed the fabric behind him as she glanced down at his trousers, her eyes growing wide at the bulge underneath them. After calming herself, she unzipped the front.

"W-wait."

She dropped her hands to her sides.

"I might not ... last." He took a deep breath and pushed the trousers down, then hooked his thumbs into his briefs. His cock sprang out, bobbing up and down, the heaviness and sensitivity nearly painful.

She let out an audible gasp, then the tip of her tongue darted out to lick at her lips.

He growled and once again carried her, this time depositing her on top of the bed.

"Stein," she moaned just before he captured her mouth again, their lips melding together perfectly like they'd been made for each other. She opened to him, offering herself to him, and he delved his tongue inside for a taste.

Her hands ran up and down his naked back, her nails teasing his skin. Pushing her back down, he made her lie back and spread her hair on the pillows as he gazed down at her.

"You look like a goddess," he rasped. "I want to worship you." Leaning down, he kissed her lips again, then trailed them down to her neck, her shoulders, and licked a path to her breasts. Fingers dug into his scalp when he suckled on a nipple and drew it deep.

"Gentle," she said, and when he loosened his lips, she sighed in pleasure. "Yes ... just like that."

He teased her some more with his tongue and mouth until she was squirming. Then, he moved to the other breast, lavishing it with the same attention.

"Stein ... please ..." Her thighs pressed together. "I need ..."

"We'll get there," he promised. "Just let me taste you. May I?"

The apples of her cheeks tinted with a fierce blush. Still, she nodded.

Thank Thor. He had been dreaming of this for a long time. Moving between her legs, he leaned down and pressed a kiss to her belly. Gently, he cupped her mound through the white silk panties, making her hips jump.

Gods, he'd never been so nervous in his life. He wanted to make this good for her.

"Don't overthink it," she said. "Just ... follow your instincts."

It was endearing how she reassured him. "Guide me. Tell me what makes you feel good." He gave each inner thigh a soft kiss. "And if you don't like something, promise me you'll say so?"

She nodded. "I promise."

With his confidence boosted, he caressed her through the silk, first running a finger up and down her sex until the fabric grew wet and she was once again squirming underneath his touch.

"Yes ... keep going."

He wanted to touch her naked skin so bad, but with the garters and stockings in the way, he wasn't sure how to take her panties off.

"Oh, just rip the damn thing off," she moaned. "Do it."

Gripping the waistband with both hands, he rent the damn thing down in two, exposing her to him. *Mother Frigga.* Unable to help himself, he leaned down and pressed his mouth to her.

"Stein!"

He licked at her, devoured her. Gods, she was sweet and heavenly and was more delicious that he could ever dream of. Still, he wasn't sure what else to do, so he followed the rhythms of her body, trying out different strokes and kisses, finding ones that made her sigh with pleasure or trying something else when she didn't respond as enthusiastically. Soon, he found the right combination until she was dripping with wetness.

Pausing, he looked up at her. "Vera, do you touch yourself? Here?"

Her teeth sank into her lower lip, and she nodded.

"Teach me how you do it."

Her hand moved between her legs, and her fingers moved to stroke her lips, teasing herself before they worked on that bud at the crest of her seam. He watched in fascination as her entire torso flushed, the color creeping up to her stomach, breasts, neck and cheeks as her breathing grew shallow. The sight aroused him so much, he moved his hips, rubbing his cock against the sheets to relieve the pressure. When she cried out and her body shook, he nearly came at the lovely sight. He bit the inner flesh of his cheeks to stop himself from spending all over the bed.

When she relaxed, he pushed her hand away. Then, crawling toward her, he moved her to her side and pressed himself along her back. Then he reached down and touched her where her fingers had been. The motions she made with her fingers had been imprinted on his brain, so he followed them. Soon, she was panting once more, her sweet plush ass rubbing against his cock. He clamped his mouth around where her shoulder met her neck, licking and sucking at the sensitive flesh. That must have sent her over the edge as he felt her tense against him.

"Stein," she moaned as she flooded his fingers with her wetness. He let her orgasm subside and her body relax.

"Are you ready?" He murmured against her skin.

"Oh yes." She turned her head to face him, her violet eyes filled with longing. "Don't make me wait any longer."

Pressing a kiss to her temple, he eased her onto her back then he moved on top of her, careful not to crush her. Spreading her thighs further apart, he positioned his hips between them and wrapped a hand around his aching cock. The blunt tip pressed against her tightness and he eased himself slowly inside her.

"Vera ..."

"Don't stop," she panted.

"I'm hurting you." He paused.

"You can't avoid it." Reaching up, she caressed his cheek. "I can take it."

Gritting his teeth, he leaned down and propped himself on his elbows. Cradling the sides of her face, he kissed her hard, then pushed with his hips all the way in, his mouth muffling her pained gasp.

Stein closed his eyes as their mouths remained fixed on each other. Gods, she was so tight and wet and hot ... he'd never felt anything like this before, and he would surely die from trying to stop himself from coming right then and there.

"It's all right," she cooed against his lips. "Just move a little."

"I don't know if I can." His heart pounded in his chest. "Just ... one second." Sucking in a big gust of air, he relaxed his spine, then his hips, then his legs.

Think of something unsexy. That was what they said, right? But for the life of him, his brain refused to comply. After all, how could he think of anything else at this moment that he'd secretly dreamed of since meeting his mate? Of course, when Vera began to buck up against him, he knew there was no stopping now.

A growl ripped from his throat and he met her hips. Small, gentle strokes at first, but at her urging, he quickened his rhythm. Sweet Freya, the pleasure spreading over his body was like a wave he couldn't stop. A knot grew at the base of his spine, tightening and growing at the same time. His body seemingly took over, thrusting deeper and faster into her. When she clasped and tightened around him, he lost control. His orgasm hit him hard and fast, and for a brief moment, he thought his soul had left his body.

When he did come back down to earth, the most heavenly thing greeted him—his mate, smiling up at him.

"Are you—"

"I'm fine." She brought him down for quick kiss. "More than fine. I'm wonderful."

"That we can agree on." With a sigh, he rolled off her, carefully withdrawing from her body. "Fuck," he cursed when she winced.

"I told you, I'm fine," she assured him. "I just need ... a moment."

He just watched as she lay there, eyes closed, her bare body on display. His cock twitched, wanting her again. *Not until she's better,* he told himself.

Stein knew he should be happy and satisfied. Then why was there still this growing tightness in his belly? The pleasure he'd felt making her his tonight had distracted him for a moment, but still, it was short-lived because he didn't quite make her his. Not fully.

The bond.

He had hoped it would have formed after they made love. Magnus didn't tell him exactly when and how it would happen, but said he would know it. And he knew it had yet to form.

Ranulf asked if he loved her. Again, he still couldn't say, but then maybe he hadn't been asking the right question—did Vera love him?

"Stop thinking so hard." Her eyes remained closed. "And come cuddle me."

How could he say no to that? So, he scooted closer to her and gathered her into his arms. She crept up his chest, laying her head on his shoulder, then let out a long sigh. And once again, everything felt right.

Just for tonight, he pushed those other thoughts away and basked in the warmth and joy of his mate's satisfied smile.

CHAPTER 11

Waking up next to someone was a new experience for Vera, especially a very male, very naked someone. But, oh gods, did it feel so good and right. She sighed and snuggled deeper against Stein's chest. He stirred, but didn't wake.

Unfortunately for Vera, she was one of those people who had a hard time going back to sleep once she woke up. The cocoon of Stein's arms was wonderful, but all she could think about was last night. *Stein and I made love.* Frankly, she didn't feel any different now that she wasn't a virgin anymore. Except maybe for that bubbling giddiness inside of her.

Feeling the call of nature, she carefully disentangled herself from Stein. She was halfway to the bathroom when she realized she was dressed in an oversized shirt. Inhaling deep, she recognized Stein's scent. *Oh.* He must have woken up in the middle of the night to put it on her. She smiled at her mate before heading into the bathroom.

After finishing her business, she decided that she needed

a hot shower to soothe the slight pain remaining between her legs. While it wasn't as bad as she'd heard, she suspected that Stein was more—much more—larger than average. Her cheeks heated at the memory of it all, but she couldn't help but smile, then shiver at the pure pleasure he'd given her.

She turned on the tap and just stood there, letting the hot water run over her. Then she heard a familiar, raspy voice.

"Good morning."

Her eyes flew open. "Good morning." For a large man, he moved silently. She didn't even notice he'd come into the room and was now standing outside the glass stall. "Join me?"

He grinned at her before stepping inside. "How are you today?"

"My, my, aren't we formal this morning?" she teased. But she understood him completely—this was a new and slightly awkward situation for both of them, after all. Wanting to put him at ease, she placed her hands over his inked chest and slid them up to his shoulders. "Kiss me."

He answered her request without any hesitation. The shower continued to rain down on them, filling the stall with steamy mist. Vera found herself pressed up against the tile wall and Stein's substantial erection brushing against her thighs.

"Oh yes," she moaned into his mouth as she rubbed against him.

He grunted. "It's too soon. You're too sore. I hurt you ..."

"No, I'm fine. I swear."

"You need time to properly heal."

"I'm not an invalid." She was a grown—and currently, very frustrated—woman.

"Vera ..."

An idea popped into her head. A very wicked idea that would have made her blush from head to toe were it not already steamy inside the shower stall. "But since you insist, I'll have to take this in another direction." Her hand snaked between them and gently grasped his cock.

The growl that came from his chest made her feel a primal power she'd never felt before.

"You know how this is done, right?" She tightened her grip.

"Yes," he answered through gritted teeth.

"Teach me how you do it," she said, echoing his words from last night.

"Vera! Ugh ... yes." His hand closed over hers and brought it down to the base of his shaft. "Start here." He assisted her with the motions, her palm moving over his cock in long strokes. "That's it ... hold it like that."

He gave her instructions in that sexy, raspy voice of his, moaning and groaning with each movement. The feel of him was fascinating and unlike anything she'd touched before. It was hard to believe he'd been inside her last night, giving her pleasure.

"Vera!" He cried out as his cock pulsed and jumped. Fingers dug into her hair and he leaned down and kissed her savagely as he thrust into her hand. Ropes of warm, sticky substance sprayed over her fingers and some landed on her belly. Sweet Freya, she didn't orgasm herself, but she nearly did. It felt so empowering, knowing that she'd done that.

Finally, he released her mouth and leaned his head against the tile behind her. "One moment." Taking a deep breath, he picked her up and then carried her, fireman style, over his shoulder.

"Stein!" she protested as the world turned upside down. "What are you doing? Where are you taking me? I'm still wet from the shower." Moments later, she found herself deposited back on the bed. "Stein ..."

"I'm going to have to pay you back, woman." He grinned at her, then grabbed her ankles and spread them apart. "I'm going to torture you, and you'll have to take it."

"Stein!"

He feasted on her again, his mouth diving between her legs. This time, he seemed to have remembered her instructions from last night as he used his lips and fingers to drive her to a quick orgasm. Soon, he was crawling between her legs again.

He made love to her, slowly, as if he had all the time in the world. The discomfort was brief, but soon, she was moaning and writhing underneath him, begging him to let her come. He prolonged their pleasure, speeding up only after he'd wrung out at least two orgasms from her before he gave in to his own orgasm.

Sated, he rolled over and gathered her to him. "That was ..."

"Amazing," she finished. Gods above, her brain was still scrambled.

They lay there in silence, basking in the afterglow, cuddled to him as he lazily stroked her arm.

"What should we do today?" she asked when she found the strength and the sense to speak.

"Whatever we want. Rorik said we can take as much time off as we want this week, as long as I can fill in if we become shorthanded."

"He said that? When?"

"Through our mind link, just a few moments ago."

"Oh. Right." Queen Sybil had told her about how the dragons could speak to each other without using words.

"What would you like to do, wife?"

She warmed again at the word. "I'd like nothing more than to stay in here with you."

"Sounds like a plan." He kissed the top of her head. "I can call the kitchens for breakfast when you're ready."

"Mm-hmm." She nuzzled his shoulder. "Oh, wait."

"What's wrong?"

She sat up. "Well, I was wondering if you wanted to go on a honeymoon or something." She frowned. "Not that I had anything planned with To—" His lips thinned, so she stopped short. "I mean, my, uh, original plan for today was to hand over the paperwork to the solicitor so he could start the process. I didn't want to wait another second. You understand, don't you?"

"Of course. Any minute a child is without protection is a minute too long."

"Oh, right. After your ... your father was put away, you were probably put in the system, right? I've heard terrible stories of what that was like before Queen Sybil started the Children's Foundation."

His pleasure-drugged eyes turned stormy, like a tempest appearing from nowhere.

She gasped. "I'm sorry. That was insensitive of me." Her chest tightened at the feeling in her gut that told her she had said the wrong thing. "Stein?"

He remained still as rock, but now his expression turned vacant. Like he wasn't even present.

"Stein?" she whispered again. "Stein, please ..."

He blinked, but his expression remained stony.

She placed a soothing hand on his chest. "Where did you go?"

Gently, he brushed her hand off and slid off the mattress. "I shall ring the kitchen for breakfast."

Vera sat there, unable to do anything but watch him disappear through the door.

Really, Vera? Did you think any man would—

Shut up!

She shut that voice away as an uncomfortable lump formed in her throat. While Stein had told her about what happened with his parents, she never did hear anything about what happened after that. It was hard to believe, but what could have been worse that seeing your father murder your mother?

Before she could even go after him, he came back.

"Breakfast is on the way," he said, slipping back into bed with her.

She looked up at him warily, and to her relief, those steel gray eyes were normal. Her mate was back. "Good." She crawled back to him. "I'm getting hungry."

Lust glazed over his face. "Me, too."

As he pushed her back on the mattress, Vera swallowed that lump in her throat. Perhaps she'd just imagined it all. Maybe there was nothing more to it than a sad story about losing his parents and being in foster care. Yeah, she told herself as she gave in to the pleasure he was giving her. That was all.

They spent the next two days cocooned in Stein's apartment, barely seeing anyone else. Anything they wanted or had to get done, the palace staff or their friends happily provided. Gideon and Ginny assisted with getting the paperwork to Liam Hartensen to start the adoption, while the kitchen prepared all the meals they needed. Queen Sybil also sent for a few of Vera's personal items to be sent over from her home.

Before Stein, Vera didn't know what all the fuss over sex was about. Her mother had barely taught her the basics, and the only instructions she had given was "just lie back and think of his bank account." She wasn't ignorant about sex and enjoyed her solo time, but sex with another person just didn't seem that great when she could bring herself to orgasm and get on with her day.

But sex with Stein was nothing like she'd imagined. Sure, they were both learning, and not everything they tried worked, but when it did ... fireworks seemed like too mild a word to describe them. The things they did made her blush just thinking about them, and one of the reasons she was reluctant to leave the blissful sex bubble of Stein's apartment was that once she emerged, *everyone* would be looking at her and know what they'd been doing.

"I hate to leave you." They stood by the door; Stein dressed in his usual Dragon Guard garb.

"Alyx and Mikhail are headed back to Paris," she reminded him. "Which means you need to go back to your duty." Rorik had been generous enough to give Stein more time off, but with Ranulf and Magnus leaving, they would need him back. "And I need to attend the goodbye lunch for Alyx and visit Lisbet."

His brows furrowed. "Are you able to wait for me to visit Lisbet? I would like to come as well."

"Y-you would?"

"She does not know me yet, so I think it would be the responsible thing to do to take the time to be around her."

Her heart got all warm and fuzzy. "Of course. I plan to go this afternoon when she comes home from school."

"I'll speak with Niklas and ask if he can relieve me earlier." He let out an unhappy grunt.

"What's wrong?" It was funny, but Vera could now interpret all the grunts and wordless sounds he made.

He glanced around him. "This place ... surely you can't be comfortable here?"

"We haven't exactly been outside the bedroom much." A fierce blush bloomed on her cheeks.

"How about we stop by your father's house, and we can take a few more of your personal things? Just so you feel more at home here. There are empty drawers in the dresser, and I can move my things so you have space in the closet. Go ahead and have a look and make any changes you want. We should also discuss where the three of us will be living permanently."

Gods, could this man be any more wonderful. "I would like that." Reaching up on her tiptoes, she brought him down for a kiss. It was meant to be a quick peck, but somehow, she ended up against the wall, legs around his waist, writhing against him.

"Stein ... you're going to be late," she panted.

An unhappy *hmmm* left his mouth, and he put her down. "I'll come find you when I'm done." After another quick kiss, he left.

Vera turned back to the living room. The emptiness left in Stein's wake was oppressing and the silence deafening. Without him, it felt like a display room of a furniture store or a hotel suite. Of course, the impersonality of the entire apartment—from the furniture to the bare walls—didn't help.

Huh.

Now that she had time to think about it, nothing in this place had any personal touches. The couch, coffee table, and even the throw pillows were the standard ones she'd seen in the palace's guest suites. *It's like he just moved in last week.* Or checked in last night. She padded into the bedroom and it was the same thing. No knick-knacks, no photos, not even pocket change or receipts lying around on tabletops.

Maybe he's just neat.

Heading toward the dresser, she paused, wondering if she would be violating his privacy if she went through them. However, she remembered he told her to go through the drawers so she began to open each one.

There was no privacy to violate in the first place. There were no personal items hidden among the neatly folded piles of shirts and underwear. It was the same for his walk-in closet. Several pairs of his uniform hung from the racks, and shiny leather boots occupied half the shoe racks. But there were no boxes with keepsakes or cherished family heirlooms. It was as if he only existed as Dragon Guard Stein, springing forth as a full adult like Athena from Zeus's head.

A sadness crept over her, but also, a nagging curiosity. Somehow, she knew it had something to do with what happened to him after he lost his parents. *I should just leave it be.* Obviously, it must have been a painful time, as the last time she'd brought it up, he practically shut down. *And shut me out.* The last couple of days had been so happy, she didn't want to spoil it.

But the thought that he was hurting over something was hard to let go. It wouldn't leave her mind, not even as she was surrounded by her friends.

"You look like you're a million miles away, Vera," Alyx teased. "Stein really rang your bell, huh?"

Queen Sybil had prepared a lunch at the royal apartments for Alyx as she was going back to Paris that afternoon. Almost everyone was there, including Alyx's family and basically everyone who had been at the wedding.

"Sorry," she said sheepishly. "I'm just ... you know, thinking about things."

"How is married life?" Ginny, Gideon's mate, asked. "I mean, I know it's only been a couple days. But you're happy, right?"

"Oh yes." She nodded enthusiastically.

"The bond really is extraordinary," Annika said. "It's like nothing I've felt before. How did you feel when yours formed?"

"Formed?" Vera sank her teeth into her lower lip. "I mean, now that we're married, we're bonded, right?"

"We're talking about the mating bond," Queen Sybil said. "The link that forms between mates. I don't know how to explain it, but it's like ... your soul is tied together. You'll be able to feel his moods like they were your own."

"And know when he's near," Poppy, Rorik's mate and fiancée, piped in. "It's wild, right?"

"Oh. I ... uh." She definitely did not feel Stein's emotions.

"The bond hasn't formed yet, has it?"

Annika's words were not a question, but a statement.

Vera suddenly felt ... lacking. All this time, when she watched her friends go through their own courtship with their mates, she thought the bond had been some kind of agreement. Like a handshake deal. She didn't expect it to be an actual metaphysical bond.

"It's not something that just happens once you guys bonk, you know." Alyx patted her hand reassuringly. "There's lots of factors involved, like you have to return each other's feelings."

"And that there's nothing blocking the bond," Annika added.

"B-blocking it?"

"Niklas and I had to work through our own insecurities and problems," the female dragon explained. "There can be no secrets between you because if you're not open and honest with each other, love cannot flow freely, and the bond won't form."

"Huh, I never thought of that way," Queen Sybil said. "But it does make sense, doesn't it? With the mate bond, you feel each other's emotions and presence. In the beginning, it's such an unnerving and raw feeling. You can't keep secrets from each other because the other will immediately know. I know that if Aleksei were to lie to me about anything, I would feel so hurt and resentful."

"I see." That pit in her stomach that had formed that morning began to grow. But it didn't make sense. He'd already confessed what sounded like his biggest secret, and so had she when she shared her childhood with her mother. What else could there be to share?

Her mind went back to the morning after their wedding. How he'd shut down. Could it have something to do with that? He didn't want to talk about his time in foster care. Perhaps something terrible happened there. Something so terrible that affected him so much, it was blocking the bond. But how would she ask him?

The questions never left her mind all afternoon. When Stein came to pick her up so they could go to the Children's Foundation, she shelved it momentarily so she could focus her attention on Lisbet. The child was ecstatic to see them and even managed to say a few words to Stein.

Later, when they arrived at her father's estate to pick up her things, she had an idea. Perhaps she could broach the subject while she packed.

"Could you get that for me?" She pointed to the shadowbox sitting on top of her dresser.

Stein grabbed the item and walked over to her. "What is it?"

She smiled up at him as she took it. "Keepsakes from my time at boarding school." Turning it to him, she pointed at each item. "That's my acceptance letter. My first report card. The corsage for my first dance." His lips pressed together and he let out an unhappy murmur. "It wasn't given to me by a boy. Everyone got one from the teachers," she explained, which seemed to appease him. "And that's the photo of me and Pappa at the graduation." Wrapping it in bubble wrap, she placed it on top of her suitcase and zipped it closed. "So ..." She cleared her throat, then turned to look at him. "Did you finish school here in Odelia or elsewhere?"

The air in the room shifted in a split second. That cold, empty stare returned. Turning on his heel, he made his way to the door. "We need another box. I shall ask your butler to fetch me one."

His sudden chilly exit left her gaping.

Did you think you could have everything you want, Vera?

No! Shut up!

Why did that voice have to come back now?

The pit in her stomach was now a yawning chasm. Vera had convinced herself what had happened the morning after the wedding had been some kind of fluke or a figment of her imagination. But no, this was the evidence that she hadn't made it up in her mind. And just as she'd suspected, it had something to do with what happened after he'd been essentially orphaned.

"I have the boxes."

She started at the sound of his raspy voice. Again, Stein looked ... normal. Like he hadn't just left the room in an arctic wake.

"Thank you." She flashed him her brightest smile and continued packing her belongings.

Later that evening when they arrived back at his apartment, it was like everything was back to normal. They made love and cuddled in bed afterward, with Stein falling asleep as Vera lay her head on his chest, listening to his breathing and his heartbeat.

Everything back to normal.

But there was something different at the same time. It was imperceptible, but it was there, nonetheless.

CHAPTER 12

Vera had fallen into an easy routine over the next week. Mornings were spent with her solicitors, gathering documents and evidence for the adoption, and then she'd head to lunch with her father. After that, she headed to the Children's Foundation to visit Lisbet and do her volunteer work. As a patron, she didn't really need to put in time at the Foundation, but she liked the work and it gave her purpose. And there were always luncheons to plan, fundraising to do, and general office work. Evenings were spent back at the palace, either with the royal family or moving more of her things into Stein's—or rather, their—apartment. And because her husband had such an erratic schedule, they would find ways to fit him into her day, whether that meant spending an extended time in bed in the morning, skipping dinner altogether, or staying up late.

For anyone looking from the outside, Vera had the perfect life, and she had everything she could wish for. And she truly did, and she was grateful. But every day, the heaviness in her grew, as did the distance between her and Stein. Not physically of course—making love with him was the most earth-shattering experience in her life. As they grew more familiar with each other, their ability to give each other pleasure increased. The physical aspect wasn't the problem. Each day that passed that the bond didn't form, Stein felt farther away. But there was no way to ask him about it without bringing up the past, and she didn't know how to do that without having him pull away from her. It was like waiting for the axe to fall. Each day, tiptoeing around him, wondering what would set him off.

And it didn't take too long.

Vera had prepared breakfast—well, she had the kitchens prepare breakfast—and waited for Stein to return after his overnight shift. She was pouring herself a cup of tea when the phone rang. Placing the pot back down on the tray, she rose and picked up receiver.

"Hello?"

"He—oh dear, the operator must have connected me to the wrong extension," the unknown male voice on the line said.

"Which extension did you asked to be transferred to?"

"To Stein. Of House Kvalheim."

"Yes, this is the correct line. He's not in right now, but he should just be finishing his shift. This is Lady Vera Solveigson, his wife."

"W-wife?" There was a shuffling of papers in the background. "Hmm ... no, there was definitely no mention of a wife."

"We were married just last week. It was, uh ..." How

could she describe it? "A last minute decision. May I ask what this is about? And who I'm speaking with?"

"Of course, apologies, my lady." The man cleared his throat. "My name is Christoffer Gothenberg, family solicitor for Jarl Otto Von Holstein."

She recognized the name; it was one of the oldest Jarl-doms in the Northern Isles, but she couldn't recall ever meeting any of the Von Holsteins. "And what business do you have with my husband?"

"My lady, Jarl Von Holstein is your husband's grandfather."

Vera had to pause. "G-grandfather?"

"Maternal grandfather," Gothenberg clarified. "Via his human mother, Lady Alma. Anyway, the jarl asked me to get in contact with his grandson."

The words sank in slowly. His mother's father was alive? Why didn't Stein mention him? "M-may I ask the reason?"

"I can't go over specifics. Privacy reasons, you see. But I can tell you that Jarl Von Holstein is gravely ill. His doctors said he may not have much time left and thus wishes to see his grandson."

Poor old man. "We will come and see him, of course. As soon as possible. Today." Still, it was strange Stein wasn't aware of his grandfather's condition. *Unless he was ...* Her stomach tied up in knots. Somehow, she knew this had some-thing to do with Stein's past and what had happened after his father was put away.

"Thank you, my lady." The solicitor sounded relieved. "Please, take down my number and call me when you are ready. The Jarl's chauffeur will pick you up."

Grabbing a pad of paper and pen by the door, Vera scribbled down the number Gothenberg rattled off then thanked him before hanging up.

"He has a grandfather." She clutched the pad to her chest. *And he didn't tell me.*

Before she could think any further, the doorknob turned. She barely had time to gather her thoughts when Stein walked inside.

"Gods help me, Niklas is getting on my—Vera?" He frowned. "You're looking pale." He marched to her side. "Are you all right?"

Finding the right words proved difficult, so she said the first thing that came to her mind. "Why didn't you tell me you had a grandfather who was still alive?"

Those dark, stormy eyes returned once more. "How did you find out?"

It stung to know that he'd been hiding it from her. "How did I find out? That's all you have to say?"

"About him, yes." His jaw hardened. "Did he find out about our wedding and try to contact your father?"

Hurt gave way to outrage. "For your information, his solicitor called here. Do you know how humiliating it was for me to learn about your grandfather's existence from a stranger? And he's a Jarl? When were you going to tell me?"

"Why? Does it make it better for you now that I come from a noble family?"

"That's a low blow and uncalled for." How dare he lash out at her? She wasn't going to stand for this. "I have never made an issue about that. Your worth isn't tied to who you're related to."

To his credit, he looked remorseful and rightly shamed at

his words. But she was too furious to let him apologize, so she cut him off when he opened his mouth. "He's dying. Your grandfather."

"Good riddance," he spat as cold rage crossed his face.

"Stein!" Who was this person before her? "How could you say that? How could you wish someone dead?"

He didn't speak, nor did he meet her gaze.

"He asked to see you," she said. "And I think we should go."

"No." The answer was clear and simple, his tone clearly stating that there would be no budging.

"You don't mean that," she whispered. "He's your only family left."

"I don't want to talk about this." He spun on his heel. "I'm leaving."

This was it. The confirmation she needed that this was the block that was preventing the bond from forming. So, she played her last card because she was done tiptoeing around the issue.

"I know about the bond." He froze as his hand reached for the doorknob. "And that it can't form if we're not open and honest with each other. You can feel it, right? The longer we're together and the bond doesn't form, it's like the farther apart we are. M-maybe this is why." She awaited his reaction, but he didn't say or do anything. But he didn't move either. "Your grandfather's solicitor is having a car sent over. I'll be at the main entrance at noon."

He let out a grunt—a new kind of grunt she couldn't quite interpret—and then yanked the door open before leaving.

Her stomach bottomed out, but she had to have faith in

him. That being mates meant more to him than having to confront the ghosts of his past. That she was worth it.

Please be there, she said silently. *Please, Stein, be there for me.*

CHAPTER 13

S tein landed on his two human feet, the force of his weight leaving deep grooves in the grassy dirt. As he looked over the Cliffs of Skruor, his dragon raged at him, sinking its teeth and claws into him. And he let it because he deserved every bit of pain for what he'd done to his mate.

His animal wasn't just furious at him for making Vera angry this morning. No, his inability to form the bond fueled his dragon's rage. His mate hit the mark with her words. They were drifting apart as each day they didn't bond passed. He did sense it, but chose to ignore it.

Because he was a godsdamned coward.

He shut his eyes, as if that would protect him from the truth.

He was afraid, pure and simple. Afraid that even after all this time, he'd turn into that scared young man who trembled in the presence of his cold, callous grandfather. Whose icy glare rendered him speechless. Whose voice still rang in his head, telling him he was worthless.

No, he refused to go to the old man. And certainly not with Vera. What would she think of him when Otto brought up the past? How would she react when he told her—and the vile old coot certainly would—about everything Stein couldn't confess himself.

Gutter rat.

Dirty delinquent.

Criminal.

His grandfather's voice rang clear as day in his head. Like it had been yesterday instead of over a decade ago.

His dragon scoffed at him. Idiot, it seemed to say. She won't care about that.

Vera's heartbreaking expression appeared in his mind. *I'll be at the main entrance at noon.* He knew what she was trying to tell him. That she wanted him to be there and to prove to her that he deserved her.

She's not for the likes of you, boy.

Don't touch, boy.

Too good for a gutter rat—

His dragon let out a fierce, thunderous roar, blocking the voice from his mind.

No!

Never again!

Opening his eyes, he stared out into the ocean, the dark blues and greens sparkling like jewels. He probably didn't deserve her, but he had to somehow make it up to her. And he would start with the truth, because he owed her that at the very least.

The sun was nearly at its highest peak, so he flew as fast as he possibly could, landing on the front lawn of the palace just in time to see the black Rolls Royce pulling up to the driveway. The look of shock, then elation of Vera's face as he materialized a few feet away from her made hope spring in his chest.

"You came," she whispered.

"For you, always," he said, though, he felt as if he had nails stuck in his throat. Before she could answer, the driver walked over to them and opened the rear passenger door, then gestured for them go in.

Stein helped Vera inside, then climbed in. Scooting closer to him, she laid her head on his shoulder. His stomach tied itself in knots. He desperately wanted to tell her everything, but the words wouldn't come. There was no way he could paint the past in any kind of positive light. She would hear it from the old man himself, and there was nothing he could do to stop him. Besides, if Vera could not accept him as he was, then the bond would not form anyway. All he could do now was enjoy what could be his last moments with her in his arms.

Though he willed time to slow down, his impending doom loomed closer as they approached the austere gates of Skeilmeir Manor, the seat of the Von Holsteins. A cold sweat broke out on his brow as the Rolls Royce crawled up the paved driveway and stopped in front of the enormous Gothic-style mansion on top of the hill.

Vera gasped as they alighted from the car, her eyes widening but said nothing. Instead, she slipped her hand into his and squeezed tight. His nerves calmed somewhat, and he led her to front door which opened before they even finished climbing up the steps.

"Master Stein," the impeccably well-dressed man in the black suit greeted, his hawk-like nose raising to the air.

"Gunter." The butler had been in the service of the Von Holsteins for decades, and extremely loyal to the jarl. Though he was coldly respectful to Stein, it was obvious he did not care for him.

His gaze flickered to Vera, then back to Stein. "Your grandfather is waiting."

They followed Gunter into the house. The dark walls covered in priceless artwork and the plush Persian carpets underneath his feet seemed to close in on him, forcing the oxygen out of his lungs. He didn't even notice how hard he gritted his teeth until Vera squeezed his hand reassuringly once more. Their mate's touch soothed both him and his dragon.

"He's inside." Gunter opened the door leading to Otto's bedroom, the loud creaking from the old hinges making Stein's ears ache.

This was it. The last possible moment he would spend with Vera before she shunned him and he never saw her again. The memories of the last few days with her would have to be enough. What would he would say to her once she decided to leave him?

Vera, he practiced in his mind. *We can stay married until the adoption goes through. But you are in no obligation to keep your vows to me.* They weren't bonded and she wasn't a shifter, after all, so it would be easy for her to find another. It pained him to admit that, but he would not stop her. He'd also ask Gideon to help find a solicitor to make sure Vera and Lisbet would be cared for should anything happen to him in the line of duty.

"Stein?" Vera's voice intruded into his thoughts.

He didn't reply but crossed the threshold into the bedroom.

"So, you're finally here." Hearing the voice out loud instead of in his head was a jarring and disorienting experience. "Come closer, boy."

Much like all those years ago when he was first brought here after his mother died and his father was put away, Stein remained frozen, his feet refusing to move. He could shift into his dragon and end the old bastard in a split second, but fear still gripped him in his presence.

Finally, Vera tugged at his hand, and they moved closer. His heart hammered in his chest as they approached the four-poster bed sitting high atop the raised platform in the middle of the room. When they stopped at the bottom of the steps, the ground beneath him shifted at the sight that greeted him.

The first time he'd seen his grandfather, Stein could clearly remember how scared he'd been. He was tall for a human, and had great hulking shoulders and a severe face. He not only looked powerful, but there was a presence about him that said this was not a man to be trifled with.

The robust and intimidating Jarl Otto Von Holstein from his memory was gone. What was left was a feeble husk of a man, withered and gray as he lay on the bed. His clothes hung off his slight frame and tubes connected to a large oxygen tank ran into his nose. Stein would have thought this was a completely different man were it not for the sharp, cold gray eyes that bore into him.

Otto let out a pained cough, then wiped his mouth. "You've grown."

He refused to play his games. "What do you want, Otto?"

"Is that any way to greet your grandfather?"

"I'm here, so say what you need to say." It took every ounce of his strength to say the words. Otto did not tolerate him talking back, after all. Back then, it didn't matter what Stein said—reasoning, explaining, apologizing—the old bastard always found fault in his words and inflict the maximum amount of damage with his replies. And so, Stein stopped speaking altogether. When he'd run away to join the Dragon Navy when he turned eighteen, it was almost a relief to be among his kind and communicate without having to open his mouth and use his vocal cords.

Otto's wrinkled mouth twisted. "As you can see, I am dying. And at my death, you will be receiving nothing. No money, no properties, not a single plate or silverware from this household. You may technically receive the title of Jarl, but it comes with nothing, and certainly not my blessing. I wanted to inform you in case you had any notion of contesting the will."

As if he wanted any part of that. He wanted nothing to do with this side of his family of either. "Fine. Goodbye then." Before he could turn to leave, Vera clutched at his arm.

His sharp silvery gaze landed on Vera. "Ah, so this is your wife."

Vera nodded and curtseyed. "My lord."

"She is perhaps the only good thing you've accomplished in your life."

Now that Stein could agree with.

"Although I recently heard of the circumstances of your nuptials." The old man started a laugh that turned into a coughing fit. Clearing his throat, he continued. "My dear, have you regretted your decision yet? Jarl Armundson would surely take you back, if only to settle the massive gambling debts his wastrel of a father left behind. Yet, Armundson's father's sins are minuscule, compared to my grandson's sperm donor."

Shock registered on Vera's face. "M-my lord?"

"Ah, I see my grandson has not informed you of his heritage. Perhaps I can enlighten you."

His mate's lips pulled back. "If you are speaking of his father, then there is no need to 'enlighten' me. I know everything."

The old man cackled. "And still you jilted—or rather, ejected—your erstwhile groom for my grandson?" His eyes narrowed at Vera. "He didn't tell you everything, did he?"

Vera blinked. "E-everything?"

A malicious smile deepened the lines on Otto's face. "Of course he didn't. But then again, he gets that from his father's side. Liars and conmen, the lot of them. That's how he wooed my only daughter into running away with him. With his serpent tongue and sweet promises. And the apple doesn't fall from the tree." The old man braced himself on the mattress to sit up. "How old were you, Stein, when your father began to include you in his schemes?"

Gutter rat.

"What age were you when you were first arrested? Nine or ten?"

Dirty delinquent.

"And that last one? The one that enraged him so bad, he took it out on my daughter and murdered her? That failed robbery that left that man in a wheelchair."

Criminal.

He scoffed. "I should have left you to rot in jail instead of paying my lawyers to have your case pleaded down."

In all honesty, Stein would have preferred it. It was better than having to live two years of his life in this hellhole.

"Well, my dear? Are you regretting your decision yet?"

Stein could not look at his mate, but her silence drove a stake into his chest confirming what he'd feared all along. That once she found out his secret, she would leave him.

"Look, boy, she is rendered speechless by your deeds."

"If I am rendered speechless, my lord," she began, her voice solid as steel, "it is not because of my husband's past, but of how loathsome and odious his grandfather is."

"Disrespectful bitch!" Spittle flew from Otto's mouth. "Boy, control your whore."

"Bastard!" Stein growled. He made a motion to lunge forward, but Vera's hand on his chest stopped him.

"You are a despicable man." Vera's voice was calm, but the underlying current was evident.

Otto's mouth gaped. "How dare you!"

"How dare *you* speak to my husband—my mate—this way?" she shot back

"I am his grandfather and can speak to him any way I want."

She marched up the platform and loomed over him. "And you think I will stand here and let you abuse him this way? He's mine. I will not let you do this to him." Vera's fury burned through those dark violet depths. "Don't you know who he is? What he's done? During the attack three years ago, he saved thousands of our citizens—including you, though I'm wishing one of those drones did strike you and your black heart off the face of the earth. You're not even worth a quarter of him. He's a hero, and every day he puts his life on the line to defend our country and king. He'll be celebrated all over the Northern Isles one day. And you? You're going to die a cold, lonely, bitter old man."

Otto's expression remained hateful and icy, but Stein didn't miss his chin tremble.

"We are done here. Good day to you." Grabbing Stein's hand, she pivoted on her heel and marched out. And since he was still in a daze over her declamation, he let her drag him out of the room and out of the gloomy mansion.

"I'm ... I can't believe I did that." She heaved a deep breath. "The way I talked to him ... a dying man." She covered her face with her hands. "I shouldn't have—"

"No!" Gently, he pried her wrists away. "But why did you say those things?"

"Isn't it obvious?" She smiled up at him. "I love you, Stein."

Stein's heartbeat stuttered. Did she just say—

"But before you reply, we need to get a few things out of the way. First, while I'm mad that you didn't tell me all of this, I can't blame you. What happened to you was terrible, but none of it was your fault. You were a just a boy. You didn't know any better."

"I keep telling myself that," he admitted. "It's true, you know, what he said. I'd been participating in my father's schemes since I was a child. Small, petty crimes at first. He'd called it training in the family business. But as I grew older ..." He swallowed hard. "That man ... he's in a wheelchair because of me." He took a deep breath. "We broke into this store. My father still had to Cloak me because my dragon had yet to manifest. But I was sloppy and let go of his hand and tripped. The shopkeeper saw me and grabbed a weapon. My father had no choice but to strike him from behind. Severed his spine." Just thinking about it opened all the wounds again. Like it had just happened yesterday. "After that, we went home to my mother and—and—he tried to beat me up because I screwed up the job. But she defended me." His mother's face swam in front of his eyes. "She would still be alive—"

"No." She tugged her wrists away and cupped his jaw. "Don't say that. Her death wasn't on you." She sucked in a breath. "Your grandfather blamed you, didn't he?"

"Not in so many words." He'd thought Otto had gotten him out of jail because he cared. No, he did it so he could torture him and make him pay for the death of his daughter. "I'm sorry, Vera. For being too much of a coward to tell you that. I didn't want to lose you, and in truth, I couldn't face it myself. And now the bond won't form because of it. I know that now. Please forgive me."

"There's nothing to be sorry for. But first, there is one thing you have to do. For me."

"Anything," he replied.

"Accept your past. It's part of what makes you who you are. Face it and never live in fear of it because it can't hurt you anymore." She slipped both hands into his. "And if you find it too difficult, you must let me know, and I'll help carry the burden with you."

He paused, grasping for the right words. Then his dragon let out a deep groan and nudged at him. "You know, I always thought my father and my grandfather destroyed my capacity to feel love."

She took a quick intake of air. "And now?"

"I love you, Vera. I always have, from the very moment I set eyes on you."

"I wish I hadn't been such a selfish and blind fool." She worried at her lower lip. "All these years we've lost. The children we could have had by now—"

His arms slipped around her and pulled her up to his chest, making her gasp. "Shush, woman," he said in a teasing tone. "What happened to accepting your past?" He raised an eyebrow at her.

"Point taken. Now"—she wrapped her arms around his neck—"kiss me, my mate."

He sought her mouth eagerly, crushing their bodies together as if it were possible to be any closer at that moment. While each time their lips met sent him into a state of elation, this time, he could not even describe it. It was as if he were experiencing a new kind of happiness, one that had his dragon soaring up into the atmosphere.

Mine, his dragon said possessively.

The bond.

How he was certain, he didn't know. But he could feel his very soul knitting into hers. One life, one heart, for now until the end.

When he finally let her go, she went limp in his arms. "Stein, that was it, right? The bond."

He sent her all his love through the new link between them. Her eyes glistened. "I never thought I could feel ..." She choked on a sob. "Oh ... it's so beautiful."

His mouth sought hers again in a soft, lush kiss. This time, he felt the same love flowing back to him, and no wonder Vera wept; the beauty of her emotions through the bond was indescribable and moisture gathered in the corner of his eyes.

"My mate," she whispered against his mouth as her hands

cradled his face and fingers wiped away the wet tracks down his cheeks. "Let's go home."

"With pleasure."

And for the first time in his life, his dragon let out a resounding rumble of contentment.

EPILOGUE

Another day, another wedding. Only this time, it wasn't Vera walking down the aisle.

"Are you sure you wouldn't have wanted something like this?" her husband asked as they made their way to the front row to join their friends.

Vera glanced around, admiring the elegantly decorated grand ballroom of the palace where Poppy and Rorik would soon be wed, followed by a reception outside on the front lawn. "It would have been nice to have had your input on decor and the cake." He grimaced, so she nudged him teasingly. "But no, I wouldn't have wed you any other way." She flashed him a grin. "Besides, think of the story we'll be able to tell our children and grandchildren someday."

The rare smile that lit up Stein's face would have indicated to anyone watching how thrilled he was at the statement, but even without it, Vera knew the thought of children filled him with so much pleasure and joy because she *felt* it. Everyone who told her about the bond was right—it was difficult to describe the feeling, the way her soul and heart were in tune and sync with his. But one thing she was sure of—there were no more secrets or doubts between them.

"Are we starting yet?" Lisbet fidgeted in her seat and scratched at the lace collar on her dress.

She smoothed away the stray lock of hair from the child's forehead. "Soon, *lilla du.*" Vera had taken care of obtaining the necessary permissions for Lisbet to join them for the day, which thankfully had been granted by the courts. However, she already dreaded bringing Lisbet back to the Children's Foundation later tonight.

"Do not worry, my mate." Steins' gravelly voice oddly soothed her. He must have sensed her anxiety through their bond. Threading his fingers through hers, he brushed her knuckles with his lips. "Soon."

Yes, soon they would have Lisbet with them, living in their apartment in the North Tower. The adoption process was proceeding quite rapidly according to Liam Hartensen and he had already put in the petition for them to gain temporary custody of Lisbet. In a few weeks, she might be living with them. Vera was already getting the spare room ready for her, but hopefully they wouldn't have to stay there too long.

King Aleksei had noticed that the North Tower was already growing crowded with the presence of mates and children, so he decided to offer alternative housing arrangements for his Dragon Guards. There were no solid plans yet, but the king promised them land and space for their families to grow.

The music began to play and so everyone settled in their seats. Rorik walked down the aisle with his father, Neils of House Asulf. Next was Wesley Baxter, who served as

Poppy's "Man of Honor," looking adorable in his formal wear. Then, the music changed. Everyone got up to welcome the bride and her parents.

What was it about weddings that made her cry? All the emotions surrounding the ceremony, this idea of pledging to be with this one person for the rest of your life through all the travails and triumphs, brought her to happy tears. To her surprise, however, the emotions warming her chest weren't just her own. Looking up at her mate, his face remained stony, but she knew better. She smiled to herself. King Aleksei was right about what he said when he married them —it was all worth it.

Once everyone settled down, the ceremony began. The love and joy between the bride and groom were evident in the way that they looked at each other. Even in the room full of people, they only had eyes for each other. Once King Aleksei—yes, when they found out he could legally marry anyone in the Northern Isles, all the engaged Dragon Guards wanted him to perform their ceremony—pronounced them man and wife, the entire ballroom applauded and cheered for the happy couple.

Later, everyone gathered in the garden for the reception, and soon the party was in full swing. Lisbet had been shy, not used to being around a lot of adults in one place, so Vera and Stein ensured she was comfortable and never made her speak to anyone she didn't want to. However, it was obvious that she desperately wanted to play with the other children as she watched them run around the dance floor.

Vera sighed sadly, wishing she had more experience with children aside from her volunteer work. She didn't even have her own childhood to draw from because she'd been raised by nannies, and when she did go to school, she'd been a stuck-up snob and a bully. Her mood plunged even more.

Stein's arm came around her reassuringly, as if saying, *I'll take care of this*. She leaned into his side, comforted by his presence.

From the other side of the ballroom, Niklas turned toward them, then to Vera's surprise, crossed the dance floor, taking the hand of two of his kids—blonde identical twins wearing matching pinafore dresses.

"Hey, Lisbet," Niklas greeted. "Have you met my girls?" He nodded to the twins. "This is Eva and Elsie. Girls, this is Lisbet."

"Hi Lisbet!" they chorused. "How old are you?" one of them—Eva, maybe—followed up.

"I-I'm seven," she replied.

Elsie grabbed her hand. "Come play with us. You should meet our brother and sister."

"She's a ferret and he's a snake," Eva added. "But don't worry, they won't hurt you. Maya's a bit bossy, but we love her anyway."

Niklas chuckled. "And once you're part of her circle, you'll have no better protector, except perhaps your pappa." He winked at Stein, who, surprisingly, did *not* glare back at the other Dragon Guard.

Lisbet looked up at her and Vera nodded. "Go on."

"Let's go!" The twins grabbed one hand each and dragged her to the dance floor where the other kids welcomed her heartily.

"Thank you," she said to Niklas.

"Don't thank me." The corner of his mouth kicked up, then his eyes darted to Stein. "Actually, I should be the one thanking you. Your mate hasn't been in a good mood since, well, ever." When high-pitched screams and wails pierced the air, he winced. "Well, that's my signal." Turning toward the dance floor, he shouted, "What did you rug rats do?"

Vera giggled as Niklas broke into a run, chasing after a furry little creature darting furiously toward the dessert table.

"Thank you," she said to Stein as she snuggled deeper into his arms. "For everything."

He responded with a grunt.

Music, food, and drink flowed freely, and once the sun set, torches were lit to keep the party going. Though she and Stein stuck together, they also mingled separately with other guests. Eventually, Vera found herself with the queen in a quiet corner away from the noise and merriment. The staff had brought out a comfy loveseat just for her due to her very advanced pregnancy.

"Can I get you anything, Your Majesty? Some water? Maybe your bunny slippers?"

"No, no." Queen Sybil gestured to an empty space beside her. "Sit. I'd rather have your company." She leaned back and sighed in pleasure. "Get this thing out of me," she half-joked. "I just want to see my baby. That, and Aleksei's driving me nuts with his overprotectiveness. Can you believe he asked—ordered—me to stay in bed today? I threatened to singe his eyebrows off if he didn't get out of my way."

"I'm sure the king is just thinking of your well-being."

The queen looked around, as if to check if anyone was listening. "We haven't told anyone yet, except for Pappa and my parents, but we're having a girl."

"A girl," Vera exclaimed. "How exciting. I'm so over the moon for you. And another female dragon."

"I'm happy and terrified at the same time," she confessed. "Not just because she'll be sought-after once she's grown. I swear, Aleksei's already sprouted a few gray hairs just thinking about suitors, and she's not even here." Her expression turned serious. "But, well, you understand. Being a woman is hard. I don't know if I'll raise her right."

"I have the same feelings, too, about raising Lisbet and any future children."

"Is it about your mother?"

Vera nodded. Before she told Stein, the queen was the only other person in the world who knew about her childhood. Back when she decided she needed to change her ways, the first thing she did was approach Queen Sybil and apologize for the way she acted. They sat down and spoke at length, and the queen forgave her, but more than that, Queen Sybil became her first true friend.

"I asked my mom for advice when I got pregnant and she replied, 'No one really gets instructions on how to raise children'," the queen said. "The best thing we can do is love them and show them by leading by example. And we moms need to stick together and help each other out."

"I agree," she added. "Please, whatever you need, whenever you need support, call me. Especially against bull-headed husbands."

Queen Sybil chuckled. "And soon, maybe I'll be the one offering you bunny slippers." She eyed Vera's belly meaningfully while she rubbed her own. "And maybe—" She gasped and then winced.

"Your Majesty!" Vera exclaimed. "What's wrong?" Oh dear ... "Is it a contraction?" Sweet Freya, was the queen going into labor?

"It's not what you think," she shook her head. "I ... I don't have time to explain." Her hands gripped the sides of the loveseat. "Help me up ... we need to get inside, now."

The urgency in the queen's voice was evident, so Vera put her questions aside and assisted the queen, then followed her as she made her way back to the palace. Vera thought they were going to the royal apartments, but to her surprise, they turned in the opposite direction. The queen seemed in a hurry, so she didn't ask where they were headed, but soon they arrived in a room filled with books.

"I'm here," the queen announced as she shuffled inside the library.

Vera followed behind and stopped just in time before she bumped into the queen. Several pairs of eyes turned their way, including her mate's. To her surprise, the king stood in the middle of the room, along with all the Dragon Guards and Annika.

"What in Odin's name are you doing here?" The king thundered as he stormed to her side. "Did you run here? I told you to take care. I'm taking you back to—"

Queen Sybil put her hand up. "Shush! I'm not an invalid. And by the way—you weren't going to call me to this 'urgent meeting,' were you? I had to hear it from Annika."

Vera couldn't help but grin at the feisty female dragon, who flashed her a wry smile. Yes, moms definitely needed to stick together.

Rorik cleared his throat. "Your Majesties, please. Everyone else has been waiting for this news."

King Aleksei's scowl didn't dissipate, but he nodded anyway. "Call him in."

Him? Vera walked over to her mate, hoping to get an

answer, but the look that passed across his face implored her to wait, which wasn't too long because in a split second, another figure materialized in the doorway.

"Your Majesties." The towering man with short-cropped blond hair and a thick beard bowed low and beat his fist over his heart. He wore the familiar Dragon Guard uniform just like the others, except his were threadbare. A large, menacing-looking sword was strapped to his side.

"Thoralf!" Gideon exclaimed. "What are you doing here? I thought you were in Antigua?"

"I was," the newcomer explained. "But I discovered something over there. Something that may finally bring us the cure to The Wand and defeat the Knights."

"What is it?" King Aleksei demanded. "Tell us."

"I promise, I will." His blond brows furrowed deeply. "But first, we must speak to Lady Willa."

Lady Willa?

"Who?" Thankfully, Annika spoke it aloud.

The king, queen, and Dragon Guards all looked at each other. "We have much to explain," the king said. "And I apologize, Lady Vera. You shouldn't have to bear this burden along with us."

The mood in the room shifted. Vera looked to her mate and felt the outrage and fury simmering in him and knew it had something to do with whoever this Lady Willa was. But the anger wasn't directed at this particular person, but rather, *for* her.

"I am your loyal subject, Your Majesties," she declared. "And your enemies are mine. My duty as a citizen of the Northern Isles is no burden." Fierce pride burst from her mate at the words, and her confidence boosted, despite her apprehension.

"You should come with us then," the queen said. "Lady Willa will need all the support we can give her."

As they all filed out of the library, Vera and Stein fell behind. "What's going to happen?" she whispered to him. "Will there be trouble?"

"Yes," he answered. "But we will prevail. I will do everything I can to defeat our enemies so all our children—and every child in the Northern Isles—will grow up without fear. This, I promise you."

And through the strength of their bond, she believed him.

Continue to the thrilling conclusion of the Dragon Guard series in the next book...

Dragon Guard Crusader

Available at your favorite online retailers!

I love hearing from readers and if you want to tell me what you think do contact me via email: alicia@ aliciamontgomeryauthor.com

ABOUT THE AUTHOR

Alicia Montgomery has always dreamed of becoming a romance novel writer. She started writing down her stories in now long-forgotten diaries and notebooks, never thinking that her dream would come true. After taking the well-worn path to a stable career, she is now plunging into the world of self-publishing.

 facebook.com/aliciamontgomeryauthor

 twitter.com/amontromance

 bookbub.com/authors/alicia-montgomery

9 781952 333330